For Naima.
A part of your story lives on in this book.

El Colibrí

THE WANDERINGS OF CHELA COATLICUE

Touring Califaztlán

Ananda Esteva

TRANSGRESS·PRESS

"When you come to a fork in the road, take it!"
Yogi Berra

"…It's a book of our true stories
True stories that can't be denied
It's more than true it actually happened
We comin rougher every time."
Gogol Bordello, "Immigraniada"

PROLOGUE

Coatlicue, [koːwaːˈtɬiːkʷe] *the one with the skirt of serpents*, is considered the mother of gods, in Aztec mythology. I am about to share one of many versions of her story, but it is true in the way any ancient story can be true: Coatlicue was magically impregnated when a ball of hummingbird feathers fell from the heavens and nestled into her chest. This fatherless conception enraged her daughter, Coyolxauhqui, who rallied her 400 siblings to attack their mother. In some versions of this legend, they decapitated Coatlicue. In others, Huitzilopochtli sprung from her womb fully grown, armed with a war club and wearing a hummingbird headdress. He defended his mother, killing Coyolxauhqui and many of her siblings. Despite Coyolxauhqui's betrayal, Coatlicue longed to see her daughter. So Huitzilopochtli then dismembered Coyolxauhqui and tossed her head and body parts into the sky, thus creating the moon.

Dear reader: these are *The Wanderings of Chela Coatlicue,* and like her namesake, there is more than one version of her history. They are written in this volume, but you as the reader co-create her stories by the choices you make. At the end of different chapters, you will stand at a crossroads where you can choose turning to one page or another, thus altering the course of Chela's journey and your experience of the book. Some choices lead to love, others give you insight and some lead to demise. Be forewarned that, if you read this book sequentially, you may find yourself in the throes of a freakish daymare where time, place and characters float around at random. If you read just a few stories, you will miss out on answers to your questions. Luckily, if you reach a dead-end and thirst for more, you can flip back to an ill-fated choice and choose again. Hiding in the last pages of this book is a guide listing page numbers where new choices and thus new adventures can be found.

"I am not going to die, I'm going home like a shooting star."

Sojourner Truth

A BIT ABOUT YOU

Your full name is Chavela Coatlicue Alvarez Santis, but people call you Chela for short. Ditching "Chavela" is fine by you. It's too long and has too many connotations. As it is, you aren't the most feminine twenty-one-year-old running the streets of Mexico City and rumor has it your gay uncle named you after Chavela Vargas, the Costa Rican lesbian singing corridos about women lost and conquered in a voice that shakes the tightest chests into tender sobbing. It doesn't help that your cousin Vanesa, straight up from the ranches of Jalisco has to comment daily, "Why don't you do something with your hair, Chavela?" And, "Can't you wear make up like a normal girl?" She's always acting like there's something wrong with you since you're not all plucked and painted like her. She has no clue about the music and the styles you're into. She had to move in with you when the NAFTA came, forcing the family farm to practically close down. No more veggies and goats. They have to grow genetically altered soybeans from now on, but won't turn a profit for a couple years. Since she can't live on soybeans alone, Vanesa moves into *your* room in your parents' flat in Tepito, in the heart of Mexico City. You suspect her parents are glad to be rid of her cuz once she gets going she won't shut up. It's not just about your looks, she's trying to dig out why you got kicked out of the most prestigious musical conservatory in México. You know it. She's trying to get you to slip and say something. She's relentless. Her voice is so high-pitched and whiney and her pro-CoverGirl tirades so repetitive…you fantasize plugging a mixing board straight into her neck to attenuate the frequency of her vocal chords so all you'd see would be an empty mouth moving with no sound. If only you could.

You're itching to break out of that tiny apartment. Now that she lives with you, you have to keep your instruments tied to the ceiling. The guitarrón, the electric and even the cracked stand-up bass all hover above your bed. Hopefully, there won't be another big earthquake any time soon. Maybe the place would seem bigger if it wasn't for the way your mother looks at you now. Like you shamed her. Like you're dirty. She doesn't know what really happened. You wish she'd look at you the way she did before, with light in her eyes. Now her eyes are flat, her gaze ajeno, like you're some stranger boarding in her home, paying by the week. When she's making dinner, you stand behind her, hoping that when she turns around she'll look at you lovingly, but all she gives you are the same flat eyes. Her food tastes flat, too, but you go through the motions: chew, swish and swallow. That's basically been your life since you got kicked out of El Conservatorio: going through the motions. Playing hardcore thrash, hip-hop and jazz with your whole soul is the only thing that helps you feel alive…that and sitting on rooftops with your best friend Pato and maybe doing some risky shit here and there, but mostly, your life is flat, flat as her eyes.

To practice your music, you covet times when Vanesa's at beauty school or you head off to Pato's place across town. You could never take the stand-up on the metro except late at night. It's too crowded. So you sling the electric bass in the soft case over your shoulder and wade through the crowds of people. If you smack people with its heavy neck, your attitude is *oh well.* No one apologizes for smacking your butt "accidentally."

Pato lives in a semi-abandoned school building over in Candelaria de los Patos with other musicians. Pato is the drummer in your band and, like you, he knows a wide variety of styles…even Middle Eastern rhythms swift-moving like wild river water. It's hard to find people to go deep with. It's all about having a danceable beat and familiar sound. You and Pato like to bust out of predictable rhythms that purely danceable songs cling to, like jazz improv, breaking free from the confines of a standard. Together, you form the rhythm section, mixing in beats and bass for a band you only imagine. Not to say there's anything wrong with your band, Los Huérfanos del D.F. You have a following with your heavy-bass hardcore ska laced with hip-hop. It's just you could do so much more if other members were willing to take musical risks.

"My soul was carried into my body by birds when I was born...
Carried by birds like angels. I remember."

Charles Mingus

INTERNET CAFÉ

A ttending El Conservatorio Internacional de Música for a couple of years as a high school student expanded your sights to different instrumentation styles, not to mention different instruments. It was the best opportunity you have had and probably ever will have in your life. After your expulsion, you and your uncle Gonzalo started collecting stringed instruments from around the world. He has a roomy flat resembling an overstocked museum. Besides instruments, he also collects fountain pens, perfume resins in fancy glass bottles, magazines from the fifties and the diaries of notorious femmes fatales.

One afternoon as you sit in an internet café in Cuatémoc where the fresas go for the higher speed connection, you begin to scan different Pepeslist ads for used instruments. This you do for fun. At first, there's nothing much that catches your eye besides the 1930s parlor guitar with elaborately painted flowers that look like skulls when you squint. Then you come across a bass that knocks your heart off rhythm. You can't figure out what's making you fawn over all the pictures, zooming in and out and in again. It's simple, imperfect, made by human hands. You have seen ancient European basses. You have seen futuristic bass guitars, all angular and minimal. You have even seen electric stand-ups in bleeding shapes like melty, Dalí paintings. But this bass almost comes alive. It looks like a woman's body to you. Then you read the description:

Collector's Item. One-of-a-kind. Believed to be the legendary "Perfumed Lady" belonging to Sugar Rivera, who had her made in honor of his favorite Mexican muse. Excellent tone. Unique harmonic convergences. Performance quality. Used for "sound healing." Scented with Black Opium. (Not recommended for people w/ scent sensitivities.) Good condition. Label says, "Hecho en Veracruz, Mex. 1976." No maker's name. 3/4 size. $2,699 OBO. Cashier's check only. No international shipping. No exceptions. Contact Mr. H. Long.

You like Rivera, a lot. You kind of wish you could be more like him and start a band where you compose the music and you make the other musicians take risks with you. Like him, you could create your own music school…start a movement and shit. You wish he were alive today. People say that some of his pieces were so complex that, even being written down, musicians couldn't play the songs right without him being there to guide them. That's the kind of stuff you wanna write one day. You find your heart is beating fast now. Your hands are trembling. What's going on? Why is this bass drawing you in? Your Papá's family is from Veracruz. You used to visit your grandmother there when she was alive. There are thousands of instruments from Veracruz floating around in the world and yet you can't peel your eyes away from this one. Something bigger is happening. After dropping your phone twice, you text Uncle Gonzalo the haps and a few minutes later he calls you back. On the phone he dips into a story that should have been told in person over booze or in front of a bonfire or from the top of an abandoned warehouse looking out upon Mexico City… but there, on the phone, frantic clicking of keys in the background… he starts telling you a family secret that rattles you like the lowest, loudest note, vibrating from your feet on up.

"Oh, my God, Chela! It must be 'genetic memory' that's calling to you now."

"Genetic what?"

"You are blood-related to her and you found this instrument, among thousands, because you happened to browse ads in the US at the very moment when this instrument became available…"

"Huh? What blood? What are you getting at?"

"I'm saying that you *feel something* when you see this bass and it's for a reason! This bass was made for your grandmother, Sálome!"

"I don't know what I'm feeling anymore. What makes you think this bass has anything to do with her?"

"Let me fill you in. Your grandmother, she knew this Rivera fellow. She knew him well. I am almost positive! You were not born yet, Chela, when she had an American lover. He would only visit two or three times a year. She was already a widow with most of her kids grown up, but it was still scandalous of course…"

"Why? Why does everything have to be a scandal with you?"

"Hello, Chela. They weren't married. He had his own wife…OK she was like his third or fourth wife, but still…I've always suspected this musician must have been Sugar Rivera. Doña Sálome did call her man Santos. I think he was about the same…"

"So, what's the big deal? Married, not married? You know almost all musicians cheat. Those are the perks. Low pay, but lots of…"

"Oh, my God, Chela. Think like the provincial side of the family, dear. Recently widowed women are not supposed to have love affairs with eccentric foreign married men, especially those who do not pass for white."

"What the fuck are you talking about?"

"When she was with your grandfather, people respected her more because she married light. It didn't help her reputation that she looked like Celia Cruz and conducted spiritual consultations with candles and drank perfume while in hypnotic trances."

"Well, I didn't come out light-skinned like you and Vanesa! So am I supposed to marry some light-skinned man so I can get respect?" You want to drop the phone right then. You can't believe your gay uncle, the one who had to relocate so he could be himself, is playing into this skin color crap.

"Can I finish my story? Anyway, he had a bass made for her, not just for her, but one that looked like her…vertical-grain fine-pored wood, yet carved with a rough hand. And…." He pauses. "The bass even *smelled* like her." You clutch the phone. You look at the pictures on the screen. You try to imagine your grandmother, standing tall, abundant with curves, long arms and strong hands. Her defiant cheekbones saying, "Just try to fuck with me and see what happens!" Then your picture morphs into an image from your repeated nightmares of your grandmother when she was sick.

You see the white lace covers drawn up to her neck. Her cheeks cave in. You feel your heart rate rising. You feel dizzy. She is very still. The only thing moving is a hummingbird tapping at the window from outside….

Then Uncle speaks, shattering your daydream. You catch your breath. "She said he would compose some gorgeous piece of music, play it while she closed her eyes, and let God put pictures in her head. Then they'd lose themselves to a world of childhood stories and philosophy. He was kind of a mystic, this guy, like her. He had a temper too, but she could harness it, funnel it into creativity…into love. That's what she told me, but…" he pauses.

"But what? Don't leave me hanging!"

"Her neighbor told me *her* version of the story one day while your grandmother was busy in town and I stayed in making tamales. She said this man would up and play some mesmerizing piece, she thought was Devil music, and then they'd make wild crazy love, very loud! Weird things would happen too. Hummingbirds would swarm around her shack while they were…"

"Hummingbirds?" Your stomach caves in. You want to vomit. "What are you talking about?"

"Just what I said. Hummingbirds. Those spastic, lovely, gaudy little creatures would gather around her home and hover there when she was having relations with that bass player."

"Is that normal?"

"Of course it's not normal. Those birds require a constant stream of nectar to keep up with all of that hovering. Stop wasting my minutes with this hummingbird detour, Chela. I need to tell you the rest." He takes a big breath before continuing. "According to the neighbor lady, Doña had enchanted that poor man, forcing him to make the journey over land just to have her. He was sick for her! Her charm let flow his musical greatness. When his wife found out, he was forbidden to see her. He was sick with some gringo disease and then died of grief. It is romantic after all. You have to..."

"Stop. Don't tell me any more! This is like a badly written telenovela! Do you really know what..."

"Telenovela or no, girl, you *have* to get that bass. It was hers. I know it was. Who else had that smell? Doña Sálome made her own perfume. If nothing else, go there and smell it for yourself. If it doesn't smell right or feel right, then walk away. Wouldn't you want a bass that was custom-made for *the* Sugar Rivera? You know you would! But more than that, this is our heritage in the hands of some American that couldn't care less..."

"You're crazy. It's just an instrument. We buy them all the time. It's not going to bring her back." You can barely spit out the last words. Your throat is tight. You feel sweat gathering at your brow. Is it just an instrument like you say?

"Chela, this bass was a piece of her life...the most secret and tender parts of it...of her. She touched it with her hands. It touched her with its vibrations. The bass can hit a person all the way to their bones. She cherished that bass, Chela. I know she did."

"Then why wasn't it at her place when she died? We were all there. I figure either someone stole it while she was on her deathbed or she didn't care about it anymore!"

"I'm hanging up now, Chela. I can't believe you would trash our family legacy like this! Just an instrument? One that could call forth animals from nature who'd rather be sucking down flowers than..."

Instead, it is you who hangs up. You run to the bathroom and lock the door. You start coughing. You cough and cough till your lunch spews down the porcelain. You wash your face and mouth, then return to the monitor and contact the seller. You tell him you might be interested. You need more information about the logistics. You don't reveal your potential personal link with this instrument. He could use that against you. Where are you going to come up with that kind of money and how on earth will you be able to travel to the United States legally without months of planning? You figure you better have him hold it for you in case somehow, miraculously, you end up in L.A. legally and in one piece.

That evening your uncle calls you back. "We can do this, Chela. I swear I'll help you get there. You can have my settlement money to buy it and pay for your expenses. We just need to figure out a way to get you to L.A. alive and kicking."

Without the details about the hummingbirds, you would have blown this off. You have a sour feeling in your stomach, making it harder to pretend this conversation never happened. You should probably try to get there somehow. You know damn well that your grandmother Sálome was linked to hummingbirds. You never told anyone about it. It's been your secret since you were seven years old, something that has weighed upon you. The memories tug at your throat, especially when it gets quiet. You hate quiet.

You imagine yourself playing this bass, making the earth quiver with the long ceremonial cries of the bow. Hummingbirds frolic about instead of killing themselves like in your dream. They are at peace. You wonder if this is the kind of instrument that could call the rain…that could make businessmen cry…and embittered lovers hold each other again. Perhaps this bass is a thing that could reach her in the spirit place. Perhaps then she could forgive you for ignoring her most desperate call for help, that too-hot day in July.

MAKING PLANS

The next day, you stop off at the same internet café. Using your uncle's Gaypal account and code, you're able to purchase the bass on a contingency that you pick it up in person within two weeks. The previous owner died and his nephew wants to sell everything and move to some tropical island and write a novel. He flat out refuses to ship it. He has other priorities.

You race over to your uncle's flat. You're aching to hear how he's going to get you to L.A., but first he has you flipping through old Mexican magazines, looking for mention of Rivera or any American bass player who may have traveled to México around that time. "Before I make you go through all that trouble, I guess we should be pretty sure it really was him."

"I thought you said you were sure."

"I am. It's just that I'm your uncle and as someone who is older than you, and I have extra responsibilities to make sure I'm not sending you across the country for no reason. Explaining this trip to your mother is going to be a real challenge."

"Don't remind me. Well let's see…this magazine talks about how Rivera frequented whorehouses in Tijuana. He was apparently very generous with the locals. Tijuana is a long way from Veracruz. He died in Cuernavaca, but under the strict care of his latest wife, Margaret. Ugh. Why can't any of these articles tell us the whole story, like was he here and then got sick or did he come here because he was sick? I mean, if he was disabled from this disease then how was he off playing music in Veracruz and having vigorous sex?"

"Don't get all tripped up by the bits of timeline, Chela. Pretend the border wasn't there. It really isn't that far to travel from Arizona or California. It's not like he had a factory job or something. He had time to follow the longings of his heart. Let's keep looking through these mags. Something will pop out at us!"

"Why don't we search on the internet like any halfway modern person?"

"When we have actual *realia* here? Don't be ridiculous! Touch these pages, Chela. This magazine was printed when Rivera was still... not just living, but vital!"

Before you know it, you end up spending too much time ogling Maria Felix's high-drama eye makeup and Agustín Lara—El Flaco de Oro—with his anguished face. "This is stupid. It's been hours and we're not making any progress!"

"I'm a visual man, Chela. This is how I work. Don't worry. I've got it all figured out. Getting there will be a breeze. You know I'm connected to all the closeted bigwigs out there. Let's just check out this last stack."

"I'm leaving. Why don't you go and..."

"OK, OK. Let me tell you what you have to do." His eyes are big and he looks very sincere. "Basically there are two ways I see you getting there in time. One is that you convince your band to arrange a tour in L.A. You would all cross the border by car. Before 9-11, all you needed would have been your Mexican passports. You could have told the border officials you're planning on going to Disneylandia or some other touristy thing. Now you'll all need visas. Once you're in L.A., find an excuse to make a pit-stop in Palos Verdes to check out our Perfumed Lady." It sounds so simple, but lots of people get denied visas and then there's the wait.

"Good idea, Tío, but by the time we get the visas, *if* we can get the visas, the two weeks will have passed and he'll have sold it to someone else."

"Oh, stop that! I have connections in the immigration office. Provided you all have your passports ready, the visas should be no problem. Just remember not to go out of your zone."

"My zone?"

"Figure out exactly where you're going, give the full addresses to the officials and then the visas will state how many miles, not kilometers, you will be able to go north of the border."

At least you all have passports. Pato has one from when his cousin got married in San Diego. The lead guitarist from your band, Fedi has one from when he was going to tour with the infamous group Bang Data, you have one from when you and your uncle went to Cuba and of course, Charlie is American. Charlie plays rhythm guitar, clarinet, sax and random percussion.

"So what's the other plan?"

"Do a solo trip. You won't have to deal with traveling with the boys. I have a friend who works for the World Bank named Javier who is going on a pleasure cruise to San Diego. You could be his personal assistant. No one will blink twice. Don't worry. Javier won't try anything. He's as gay as they come. Besides, he needs you as his beard. He's not out at work and he thinks some of his people will be on board."

Gonzalo's plans dizzy your head. Before you know it you've picked apart your favorite Panteón Rococó patch on your jean jacket.

"Enough information. Let's eat!"

You head over to the corner restaurant and chow on some carne asada sandwiches and slam two bottles of Bohemia beer. You pay.

Later, you drag yourself home. Lucky for you, Vanesa is at a party. The outfits she decided not to wear she dumped on your bed. You toss them in a wrinkled heap onto her bed and sit on yours thinking.

DIVINATION

You wish your tío could be the family hero and get the bass himself. He's a much better talker than you are. He knows how things work, but his passport has been revoked. Long story. You find yourself sitting at the small chair next to your bed holding the guitarrón. You run your fingers slowly up the strings, then down, not making much of a sound. Even it if was her bass, Abuela Sálome probably wouldn't care if you get it back. There must be a valid reason she did not have it when she died. You've decided. You're not going. You put your fingers in position to play the guitarrón when you think you see something out of the corner of your left eye. Your abuela used to say the left side is where death lingers...so pay attention to aberrations. Fuck it. You play the opening notes to "Cucurrucucú Paloma" and you see it again. It is small and green and dark. You place the instrument on your bed then turn your head slowly, very slowly, to the left. In that moment, while it's still in the corner almost to the front of your vision, you see it: a hummingbird. Then it evaporates. Your stomach jumbles up. You let out a sigh. "Fine! I'm going!"

You rummage through your bottom drawer and pull out the divination stones Abuela Sálome had given you: three small river stones, white, black and rose colored. You're supposed to choose either the white or black stone to represent the yes and no to a question and throw. Whichever stone ends up closer to the rose colored stone, indicates your answer. You ask out loud, "Should I go on tour to California?" You take a breath. You close your eyes. You throw. The black stone practically hugs the rosy one while the white rolls under the bed. The answer *appears* to be no…wait, you didn't choose which stone was which and you didn't put your heart into it. You poke your head out the window and call out her name. "Sálome." You wait for divine intervention. No answer. This is stupid. The dead only give clues in the movies and in folk stories from like one hundred years ago.

TOURING CALIFAZTLÁN

Y ou decide black means yes. Your grandmother Sálome used to say something about life on earth emerging from darkness like out of some ubiquitous womb.

Convincing your band members is harder and easier than you expect. First you go to Pato. "What would you say if I could book us a tour in California?"

"What the fuck, Chela? What does California have that we don't? That's the American Myth, Chela. I thought you didn't buy into those fantasies." He clicks his tongue against the back of his teeth. "We've got plenty of gigs starting in two months like the one with El Vuh. I heard that Ska-P is going to come down here from Spain and they might headline. We gotta practice like mad to get tight again. Besides, crossing the border es una fregadera. Who wants to be treated like an animal by some border pig or have something go wrong and we fall into the clutches of some coyote? Even with your sheltered life, you gotta know what they do to women in the borderlands, Chela. The narcos run all that anyway. I'm just curious how exactly you're planning on getting us to los Estados Uniditos?"

You're tongue-tied for several moments. His arguments are solid.

No room to wiggle in. Bit by bit you start to tell him the truth like a faith-healer pulling out little cancers from your gut.

"That sounds crazy, Chela. Your family is full of crazy ass stories... you all are some impulsive sons of bitches!" You feel your shoulders sink. "But my family would top yours any day...I just don't talk about our business as much as you do. But I don't know, Chela..."

"Besides helping me restore my family inheritance, are you trying to tell me that playing in a big-time club in L.A. and maybe getting signed doesn't sound enticing?"

"Which club?"

"There's so many to choose from: The Stine, Parker Street Punks, The Pulse..."

"So we're not actually booked then."

"Not yet. I wanted to consult with you first."

He sighs and crosses his arms. "I vote for The Stine, but I bet you Fedi is gonna want to play at The Pulse. Fedi is like a prima donna now. You know we'd need to invite the agents *ahead* of time...get our press-kits together and all of that!"

"Most definitely." You try to hold back your smile.

"And we gotta get visas. No fucking around with crossing the border."

Back in the day, your second cousin Walter from Jalisco crossed the border on foot knowing two words of English. Being the güero of the family, naturally blond and blue-eyed, people did not expect him to be illegal, as if the darker you were, the less likely you'd be to speak English or have proper documentation. What a joke! When they asked him for his citizenship, he replied "U.S." and they let him cross without a second glance! But that was a long time ago.

"Look, Pato, I'll book the shows if you make sure everyone has both passports and visas. I'll even get the owner of The Pulse to send us a letter that we're gonna perform at his club."

"You don't even have a gig there yet and you're already acting as if you do! It's super hard to get to play there, you know. I tried in the past and they weren't interested."

"I think we can do it. Fedi was almost a rock star last spring… people really know about him now. That's gotta count for something."

"Yeah, it does count for something, Chela. That he thinks he's all that!"

You both chuckle.

"Let my uncle sweet-talk his buddies at the immigration office to get visas for you and Fedi. We'll get all punked out and no one will confuse us for the normal people crossing the border. As long as we're spiky but clean, we'll look like the spoiled chilangos we are!"

"Talk for yourself! You're the one with both parents living…and Charlie of course."

You look down. He's right, you do have both of your parents and even if they fight, it's better than having no parents at all.

"Hey Chela, I have some connections in L.A. I'll help get us some gigs and places to crash. We can do this! Let's snatch some booty back from the gabachos!"

According to your plan, Charlie will drive his dark blue Subaru station wagon, sporting his American driver's license and switch out to American plates once you cross the border. The vehicle was a gift from his parents in the States back when he was in college. Though Charlie swears he doesn't plan to return to the US *ever*, you bet he kept those plates safe.

Pato and Fedi don't speak much English, so you and Charlie will do the talking and give off airs of importance and try to pull off a little of what old cousin Walter did. It's been done. Ideally having the visas should allow you to avoid this entire charade, but you never know when a border agent will decide to find fault with your paperwork.

There's also the timing to consider. With so many Mexicans working and shopping in the U.S., the border is totally backed up in Tijuana. Maybe trying to cross during one of the rush hours would work. The agents would be burnt—out in the late summer heat and just let you on through, even if something did smell wrong. Too bad you didn't have one of those "frequent flier" border crossing passes. Those might only be for people who live in northern México near the border. It's not like any of you plan to commute to San Diego from Mexico City.

TÊTE-À-TÊTE

You and Pato spend the next day at the internet and phone cafés rigging your gigs. Los Huérfanos del D.F. actually has some pull in L.A., who knew? Clearly getting the gigs was going to be easier than *getting to* the gigs. Now to convince the band. Charlie is easy to sway since he wishes he were a born-and-raised Mexican. He's just as cool as any real mexicano, but he doesn't see that. So all you gotta do is pull the "do this or be a gabacho" thing and he'll be eating out of your hands. The problem with Fedi is he doesn't have anything to prove…in fact, he had already proved his street cred by growing up in a población shantytown, on the newest outskirts of Mexico City…and he finished high school…and he worked at a music store…but best of all, he played with Bang Data when Joselo was sick! Everywhere he goes it's, "Aren't you the street kid who ended up playing with Bang Data?" They wrote stories about him in a bunch of magazines with titles like "Boy from The Barrio Makes Good" and "From Gun Slinging, To Guitar Slinging." Fedi is gonna be hard to convince.

First you tell him about all the great gigs you got. He raises an eyebrow—good sign—then cocks his head to the side as if to say, "What's the catch?" You were never the gig-getter of the bunch. That was either his or Pato's specialty. You had a rep for being lazy for anything besides your music or whatever fool's errand your uncle Gonzalo sent you on.

"What about *the process* you wanted to follow? We didn't agree as a band before you confirmed these gigs!" Fedi whines.

Your stomach twists up in knots.

He continues, "I could have gotten us a whole mess of gigs in all the resort towns and we coulda been eating lobster and downing the finest tequila, but I didn't get to book jack because I was trying to follow *the process.* Then you couldn't make it to the meetings at the last minute so we didn't make quorum and I had to cancel with all those clubs, making me look like an idiot! This is all so fast. Too fast, Chavela. Let's talk about it during our meeting *next month.*"

"Look Fedi, I know I screwed up. I did. But this is for a noble cause."

Fedi starts to smirk. You hunch up your shoulders figuring he's about to craft the nastiest insult and spit it out slowly so that every syllable hurts, but all he says is, "Aaah. Keep it rollin', Cha-ve-la."

"Well..." You go on about how Rivera was such a bottom dog. He played cello in high school, but no one would hire a Black man to play cello back then so he traded in his cello for a bass and taught himself to play. In a snap he turned into this genius composer innovator guy mastering jazz, bebop, classical and blues and swirling it all together in a mathematical vortex. He created his own jazz school and his own movement. He even tried to make his own label when the fat cats tried to cheat him out of his money, him and all the black musicians. He fought back. Hard. And now you want to protect his legacy. You want to snatch back a bass that was stolen from México...a bass like no other to reclaim for the Mexican people! He gives you a look. He must really think you're bonkers. Then you serve it up like the dude who now has the bass is some evil appropriator planning for the day Baja California joins the USA so he can buy a bunch of resorts and make hella more money. You don't tell him about your personal ties to this bass. You don't tell him the story about your grandmother. The whole story has burrowed deep inside you. You've never told anyone, not even Tío. You just focus on the fallen hero Rivera part. Besides, Sugar Rivera was a man and it doesn't seem like Fedi, on any kind of significant level, respects women. Then, just when he thinks your argument is over, you throw in the part about landing a gig at The Pulse in L.A.

Fedi doesn't say a word. He starts polishing his guitar meticulously. After some time, he looks up at you and says, "OK, OK, Chela, but don't expect me to do shit and yo, don't go upstaging me like you did in Coyoacán." He demands you stay behind him except during your few *official* solos. "No crazy improv. No Chela-is-the-star-bassist surprise solos taking two hours…No way!"

Two days later, you meet with Pato and he presents you with everyone's passports and visas. Everyone's except his own. "You got yours, right?"

"Oh, yeah, I just brought Fedi's. I had to go with him to the immigration office, of course. He didn't know what to do or say, but it worked out in the end. Don't worry, mine's at home in a safe place." You don't question this because Pato is the organized one. He's kind of like the papa of the group. He is twenty-seven. He's tall and meaty and he has a dense, black goatee making him look way older than the rest of you. "Anyway, let me tell you the deal with this visa thing. We can't go north of Ventura County. That's near L.A. where Magic Mountain is. If we're caught north of Ventura, we're screwed…except for Carlitos, but then again, they might try to pin some harboring illegals charge on him."

"But we're not illegals. We have visas!"

"I'm trying to tell you if we cross north of Ventura County, we're just a bunch of pinche wetbacks to them. Nowadays that means we're breaking the law, you feel me?"

"Dang, that's crazy!"

"Whoever swears it's not a crazy world out there is downing some head-shrinker cocktail. A que sí?" At that, he opens up a beer and hands it to you before opening one for himself.

By the following day, the four of you set off in Charlie's mom's midnight blue Subaru station wagon. It's punked out with your band logo spray-painted across both side doors. At least it's a four-wheel drive vehicle. You never know when you may need to off-road it these days with all los narcotraficantes running the roads…if that's who's really responsible for all the car-jackings and kidnappings. Toll roads in México are monitored by Los Federales. They're supposed to ensure no car-jacking and they take care of you in case of an accident. The problem is that the toll roads cost money, which is OK for a small outing, but for a road trip of more than one thousand miles, it adds up.

You're barely sitting in the parked car when the first conflict emerges. Pato wants to take the 15D because the road snakes about less, but Fedi wants to take the 15 because he can stop by his favorite custom guitar shop and pick up an acoustic.

"Look," says Pato. "I've been partying all night. Trust me you don't want me hurling in the car while I'm driving."

"I need that guitar, man. I already called El Mago and told him I was going to pick it up. It's made of rosewood, the same wood they used to make rosaries out of." They keep bickering on and on. You look over at Carlitos hoping he'll say something to put an end to it, but he just looks at you with his different-colored eyes, the green one flashing in the ambient light like a cat's-eye. He never stands up to Fedi. It's like he's a devotee or something.

You start to play games on your phone to tune them out. Then you decide to go for texting Tío Gonzalo; you shouldn't have roaming text overages yet. You start off with, "Guess who's being the drama queen?" and push Send. Your text bounces back. A message pops up on the screen: "You are unable to use this function." What? So then you decide to call him. The message pops up again. You throw the phone into your shoulder bag and look up. "God dammit, can't we get it on the way back?" You ask. Fedi doesn't know how pressed you are for time and if anyone is going to stop off and run an errand, it should be you. Then again you can't afford to alienate him either. He's your lead guitarist and he has clout. He doesn't need you for fame.

Pato is looking pale. Driving five days with "eau de vomit" does not sound appealing.

If you choose Fedi's route via Morelia to El Mago's guitars, turn to page 24.

If you choose to piss off Fedi, but at avoid vomit, take the low road, turn to page 28.

ROUTE 15, EL MAGO'S GUITARS

(continued from "Tête-À-Tête")

Getting out of Mexico City is like getting stuck in some cosmic loop where you wake up starting the day over and over again like in the movies. The brown haze in the sky lingers on so much farther than the city limits.

"This place needs a good rain," Charlie comments.

Before you know it you're already meandering in the foothills on your way to Paracho. Everyone knows the story. Years ago a benevolent Spanish Bishop, Vasco de Quiroga, organized the Natives so that each little region near Morelia began specializing in its own craft. That way, communities would not compete against each other. Prices could be made livable. Longevity and pride bloomed.

Fedi wants his special rosewood guitar. No other place will do. By the time you reach the general area, the sun is drooping low in the sky. Fedi is behind the wheel and steers onto a side road to find the particular, out-of-the-way guitar shop of this legendary "El Mago." He couldn't have a shop on Aquiles Serdán Avenue like all the others. No, "El Mago" had to set himself apart, to break the collective spirit of the town there. Some say he doesn't want the bad energy associated with a joint market place. They say he believes his instruments are so superior that they are at risk from mal de ojo, the evil eye. Better to have a place that's hard to find and let his notoriety draw in the buyers. He ditched the Native ways of mutual support to become a solo artist, a move many hope will not be contagious. A town of competing luthiers would break the spirit that Vasco de

Quiroga helped to institutionalize. Even before he came along, the name Paracho meant *offering*—not *hoarding*—in Chichimeca.

"What the fuck? Why does your boy have to be all the way out here?" demands Pato.

"Hey, lay off." Charlie was always down for Fedi. "That bass *you* all want so bad was probably made in some obscure place like this by some eccentric luthier."

"I don't know," you say. "It just says made in Veracruz. That's not much to go on." You notice your shoulders hunching.

"See, Chela, we have twin quests, in lak'ech yo!" You don't know whether or not he's making fun of you. "Slap down some of that Mingus dude. All this talk is trifling!"

"OK." You pause and then fumble for your CD case. "What genre do you want? I mean he had like film noir mobster jazz, Ellington orchestrations, bebop…"

"None of that bebop shit! Give me something badassed."

You try to jive with his fighting spirit. "There's like three versions of this piece. This is the previously censored version." You throw in "Original Faubus Fables," an experimental piece, possibly a tweaked version of the safer, musically tight "Fables of Faubus," but who's to say which one he wrote first?

Mingus' own words jeer out in a thick desperate tongue:

Oh, Lord, don't let 'em shoot us!
Oh, Lord, don't let 'em stab us!
Oh, Lord, don't let 'em tar and feather us!
Oh, Lord, no more swastikas!
Oh, Lord, no more Ku Klux Klan!
Name me someone who's ridiculous, Dannie.
Governor Faubus!
Why is he so sick and ridiculous?
He won't permit integrated schools.
Then he's a fool!…

The music waves about like underwater plants in a storm. After a while, Fedi interrupts the song.

"What are they all angry about?"

"The governor of one of those southern states wouldn't let blacks enter a white high school. That was Faubus."

"Sounds like the name of a bean or some shit!" remarks Fedi. "The music is too out-there for my tastes, but the message is righteous. This shit is happening all over again, anyway!"

"Here in México, you can go to any school you want to, right?" asks Charlie.

"Well yeah, but you have to pay for it and not just the tuition, the uniforms, the books, the supplies, the mandatory fieldtrips, *everything!*"

"Yeah, dude, it's like the only chance a brown kid has to enter those high-flown schools is if their dad is a narco," Fedi pipes in.

"Haven't you noticed, Charlie, how color and class line run together around here?" adds Pato.

"Yeah, yeah, but…forgot it!"

It's dark now and you're really in the sticks. Stars stand out like a scattering of magic silver seeds. "Are you sure you know how to find this place?" Pato asks.

"Sure, sure. This is how the road goes. It's just not direct." Fedi insists.

"Not direct, this is like a labyrinth n shit. We can't find anything in the dark," Pato continues.

"I know the way, pendejo. Fuckin' chill out!"

Even Charlie sets in against Fedi's piloting. "Let's just get back to the main road…any main road. This is ridiculous man!" At that, you hear a popping sound, then the station wagon rumbles and tilts to the right.

"Stop the car now, Fedi!"

He does. The tire is busted and the rim of the front right wheel is bent.

Damn!

Voices tangle and surge.

We're fucked!

Your band mates are at each other's throats.

Your fault…no, your *fucking fault!* You put your hands tight over your ears.

They must be blaming both Fedi and you: you, for concocting this whole last-minute tour. You're somewhere near artisan country. There isn't a reliable car mechanic for miles. You would have to spend the night, then hitchhike, ask around, filter through the scam artists. What a fucking nightmare! You can't fix the Subaru in time to meet up with your bass in Los Angeles! You decide to get the hell out of there and find your own way, do your solo act.

———————

Turn to page 36.

THE LOW ROAD

(continued from "Tête-À-Tête")

Who would have thought that taking the low road would make you *feel* low, too? Fedi is so bummed. He doesn't believe you're intending to stop in Paracho on the way back. Fedi doesn't believe in anything he can't see. The hood taught him that. Who's to say he's wrong?

Once you get on the 15D, the road is wide and dull. Even the hills overlooking it seem to slouch. The sunset hangs limp in the sky. Yet your car shoots through the mire. You pass your fourth toll before anybody says much. Fedi's got his wallet tucked away, tight. It's your turn to pay again. Fine, whatever. As you start gaining speed, a cluster of Federales come out of nowhere and surround the vehicle. Pato pulls over to the side. What else can he do? These guys have automatic weapons.

You're sitting up front with Pato. You promptly take over the conversation. Los Federales want to know what kind of music you play. You start in on the laundry list of different music genres. You perk up just thinking of all the styles you've mastered. Yes, sure you play traditional tunes. You figure this is a way to bond with these guys. They're probably from the rancho like half your family. The next thing you know, you're facing a bizarre choice. Either play for the captain's daughter's quinceañera now or "Handle things *another* way." What do they mean by that? If you play the quinceañera, you'll probably lose eight hours, getting there, performing, resting and then getting back to the freeway—maybe more! And some or all of you will end up drinking so you'll have to drive a bunch of snoring drunks with bad breath. Then again, what if you don't play for the party? What will they do? These are Los Federales. They don't fuck around. The captain is looking at you. It's your decision. You don't have time for some whiny group discussion, while these guys get trigger happy. The captain drums his fingers on the open window sill. Maybe he expects you to pay a bribe if you don't play for his stupid party. You could use some of Tío Gonzalo's settlement money right about now. Wouldn't it be funny if Los Federales started taking credit cards? Lord knows they get a lot of bribes and confiscate a bunch of loot.

If you decide to cooperate with Los Federales and play the quinceañera gig, turn to page 30.

If you decide to find out what "handling things *another* way" means, turn to page 33.

QUINCEAÑERA

(continued from "The Low Road")

I t looks like the captain rented out a Moorish palace for his daughter's party. You see white walls detailed with ornate, painted blue tiles. Towers with puffed up merengue spires decorate the sky. A group of five Federales leads you out to the great patio where three hundred plus people are partying. A DJ clumsily mixes CDs. His fades between songs are jagged. It's good enough. The mariachis that played at the very beginning of the party are long gone. The family wants old-school cumbias, modern cumbias, Colombian cumbias from the 80s, grupero, Los Bukis covers, lots of Los Players and a few romantic numbers, mostly boleros. You and your band huddle and come up with a play list, something you could almost live with, and only feel embarrassed through your skin, not all the way down to your bones.

You start playing, like you're going through the motions. You wonder what happened to the original band they had lined up. Did they get kidnapped and forced to play for someone else's party? Did one of their members offend the captain and get stashed away in a prison somewhere? After playing non-stop for two hours, you finally get a break. People are good and drunk by now. No fights. Not yet. You manage to mingle in the crowd. There amongst all the clones, you find a woman who resembles a man playing the role of a female opera singer. She has a faux queen, Lady Gaga, María Félix look to her like someone Tío Gonzalo would know. She's probably an art collector or some crazy good dancer, or she owns a theater company.

"Excuse me."

"Hi, my dear. Good show, although I can tell you have different aspirations. What sort of music do you *usually* play?"

"Well, I was trained in mariachi and son jarocho from my family, but I also learned classical and jazz at school and I play in a hardcore band with a hip-hop twist."

"Hardcore? I'm not familiar with that genre of music. I must not be as with it as I had hoped."

"Sure you are! It's just that I'm from el D.F...there, everyone has their thing...specific kind of music they like. Hardcore is like rock with strong driving beats and bass."

"I see. Well, I must say your cumbias do have an edge to them. Get us going a lot better than Los Players cover bands would have. I imagine the band they had lined up, Los Costeños would have played in a more generic fashion."

"What happened to them anyhow?"

"The main singer never showed up, and he was the only one who could carry a tune. Plus, he was a real looker. A heartthrob. Typical womanizer, roaming like some sex crazed alley cat. Rumor has it he got some young young girl pregnant and then coerced her into having an abortion. Her family was seriously religious and her uncle, some kind of narco enforcer no less."

Suddenly you hear feedback on the mic. They're trying to call you back. You sigh and drag yourself up there.

After another two and a half hours of playing, the party finally winds down. There was only one fight, one broken heel, one ankle sprain and two major wardrobe malfunctions involving the revelation of formerly private female body parts. You wonder if these momentary flashings of flesh were truly *accidental.*

Charlie trots up all giddy and grinning, saying that some of the guests of Los Federales are narcotraficantes, the very people they are supposed to be tracking down. To which you reply in a matter-of-fact kind of tone, "They're all middle class or rich, aren't they? Their kids probably go to the same private schools and Karate lessons."

The rest of the band members trickle in. Just as you suspected, you're the only one of the bunch who's not shit-faced drunk. So you could be either the straight laced responsible one and herd these cats on the path to the "Perfumed Lady," or you could join 'em. Hmmm. What would Abuelita do? Should you fetch the divination stones? Nah! Tomorrow…tomorrow you'll hit the road. Tonight was too surreal to stay sober.

"Hey, Charlie, get me some tequila."

———————⌒———————

Turn to page 44.

HANDLING THINGS *ANOTHER* WAY
(continued from "The Low Road")

You look back. Fedi and Charlie have sloth mouths, too slow to form words. Pato sports an expression you can't read. His eyes are wide, but he won't say anything, not even whisper. The tapping of the captain's fingers on the sill pluck on your nerves. Finally, you spit out, "As much as we'd love to play for your function, sir, we are already late for our own show in Tijuana." Not true, but it sounded good.

You can't fucking believe it! In a snap, they drag you out of your station wagon, cuff you with zip ties and throw you into the back of a van. The Subaru—punked out spray paint job and all—has been confiscated with all of your equipment and luggage and wallets. What the fuck?

"OK, OK. We change our minds. Sure we'll play for you!"

"Too late you pinche fresa wannabe roquera!"

Their insults hit hard. True you weren't from the streets, not like Fedi. But you weren't exactly a fresa, some rich, mindless fashion clone. You're original. But what do they know? These guys in these government thug jobs can't think themselves out of a barn. If only you could speak to the captain!

After several hours of being held in a small empty room sitting on the cement floor, enduring cycles of insults followed by darkness, your thirst creeps up and screams in your face. Should you ask for water? Should you bother? Charlie does and they beat him upside the head. Next thing you know you're being dragged off and into one van, while your friends are shoveled into another. Shit, how are you going to keep in contact? How is your family going to find you? Why can't you stay with them? That's right, you're the only female. You're in the van, tied up, alone, that is alone from anyone who'd treat you like a human being with rights. Let's start with the right to your own body. You're losing that right as they throw you on your face. You're losing that right as they sink fingers into your flesh and squeeze tight to hold you down. A small trail of blood trickles from your mouth and onto the van floor. That's how they'll find you, like those fairy tales of children lost in the forest throwing breadcrumbs. You will leave blood crumbs…someone will find them.… They will.

The rest of what they do to you seems so far away…ajeno. English has no word for it. The body isn't yours, but a mannequin you see in some drunken daydream. You become only the idea of a body, an abstract notion, like a long and twisted math problem, a string logic twirling and imploding on itself. When you get to the end of that problem—so long that you had pages and pages of figuring—when you get to the end, they will have stopped and maybe then you will be able to call upon your body again. You can only hope your body won't feel ajeno to yourself forever. You can only hope it will come to recognize you and let your breath run through the lungs you once knew and let the blood to run laps along your veins instead of trickling behind you, trapping you in a zombie existence. A life of gray skin and shallow breathing.

When they finish, it hurts to sit, to lie down, but you feel too dizzy to stand. Soon you *have* to stand because the cell surrounding your dizzy distant body is too full of other prisoners to allow everyone to lie or even sit at once. You lean your hand against the cool brick wall and rejoice that you can at least feel the damp coldness of it. You can feel. You can.

No one tells you your crime or how long you will be locked up. No phone calls allowed. No courtroom. No witnesses. No one knows where you are. You are one of many daughters disappeared there in that jail cell. That jail is one of many where women disappear.

———————⌣———————

This is a dead end.

Turn back to an earlier page and choose another path.

THESE BOOTS

(continued from "Route 15, El Mago's Guitars")

You step along the road alone, truly alone. You forgot your fucking guitar! No one even notices you separate yourself from the group. Pato and you have a connection like twins. You'd think he'd feel you leaving. Maybe you're not so much different from that El Mago character. Maybe you're a natural loner. The stars pulsate above, harmonizing with flashing lights. Visual music. You look back down at the road. You hear nothing, but your own footsteps. No one calls your name! No feet trotting toward you! The next thing you know you start running down the road. Then you remember your uncle José told you not to run along the side of the road early in the night. There are snakes basking in the warmth of the tarmac and snakes curling up for the night in the roadside grass. You change course and run in the middle of the road, hoping drivers have working headlights. This is México after all.

Coming from Mexico City, you're used to a human buzz 24-7: to people chit-chatting, arguing, to horns honking and the hum of the metro below. This place is so dark and quiet that your breathing sounds like a giant's. Your feet sound like sledgehammers. At the same time, you are nothing in the vastness of the night. The dark and quiet have you outnumbered and the greatness of all your noise is a pipe dream, something you cling to. You need to feel big.

Then up ahead, you notice a glimmer. You stop running and walk toward it. You find yourself tiptoeing. You notice a fluttering sensation over your head like a bird's wing fanning you. You keep walking getting dizzier as you go. Before you know it, you're on a dirt path leaving the road behind. Up ahead, the source of the glimmer reveals itself. There is a campfire and a primitive oven of sorts. As you step closer, a middle-aged woman wearing a red rebozo greets you. Her sunken heavy-lidded eyes give the appearance she's looking at some faraway place.

"My daughter, we have finished with our temascal, but you may join us for a meal now if you'd wish."

Stunned, you plop down by the campfire and a younger woman hands you an earthenware bowl full of vegetable soup, the kind of soup that no cookbook can imitate. The chiles, the potatoes, the tomatoes, the achiote and the squash blossoms have all been handled with intention, adding to the broth in ways you can't explain, but the warmth in your chest knows so well. The tortillas served with the soup are thick and hand-patted. There are four women in all, each gorgeous in her own earth mama kind of way. Two wear long braids and another has her hair cropped like a boy and the first woman who spoke to you has striking silver tresses free-flowing down her shoulders. They introduce themselves, but their names slip through your mind unheard except for the silver-haired woman. Her name is Doña Estela, meaning "tail of a comet." You like her. One of the others asks if you had been to a temascal before. You say no, but your grandmother Sálome had. The woman looks at Doña Estela. They both nod.

"Usually we never go into the temascal on a full stomach, but fortunately we haven't eaten much yet and Lidia will keep the food warm while we're inside. I think the temascal could help you right now, so we will add another round." At that, Estela holds out her hand. You take it and she leads you onto your knees to enter the temascal followed by the braided ladies. You fall into their arms as if they were always there to hold you. Inside the temascal Estela starts singing. You don't know these words. A woman whacks you with plants and rubs you with aloe. You sink down into the mud floor, her singing breezing through your mind.

You find yourself at your grandmother's home. Sálome is preparing fresh tamales, grinding sweet corn, cutting onions and then mincing an armload of hot peppers. Her tamales always had a bite. Just like her, go figure. It's almost Christmas. You catch a view of the next room from the kitchen. Her house is small with wide doorways, always making you feel close to whatever family or buddies happen by. In the next room you catch a glimpse of what you hope is a bass. You see a bowed, cinnamon colored wooden vessel. Could it be a fancy hatbox? A rounded footlocker, or could it be her? *You smell your grandmother's sharp copal smoke.*

You wake up. You're in the temascal with these ladies. *They're* burning copal, not your grandma. You clutch your toes in resistance to the metaphysical mumbo-jumbo you just fell into. But after some time, you find yourself drifting in and out of their words again… their songs…their mists…their heat…then slowly you crawl out into the night air. You tremble. Your body feels soft and half-baked. The shorthaired woman covers you in blankets and instructs you not to cool off too quickly. "You could warp your bones, you know."

Later you dress and rejoin them along the fire. You keep eating and find the more you eat, the whole drama with your bandmates disappears as if all you ever knew was this place. In your gut you hold the memory of your quest to find the Perfumed Lady. You can't let her slip by you, like you have with everything else. Estela hands you a little wooden Tarahumara doll with a red headband.

"Take this, my daughter, for safe passage in the northern lands. Sadly, I think you will need it. There are many men who have lost their sense of honor toward women and children. Watch out for them and do not trust." At that, she mumbles a prayer and gives you a hug. She also gives you a plastic bag of taquitos her neighbor made. The younger one trots up and hands you a tourist guitar. It's kind of junky, but you sling it tenderly over your shoulder. How did they know?

———————⌇◠⌇———————

Turn to page 39.

WALKING

(continued from "These Boots")

You return to the road and start walking. You know you should save them for later, but start eating the taquitos one by one as you walk. A survivor would save them for later, but your stomach is driving the show. You see headlights down the road coming your way. Could it be your band? As the vehicle rolls up, you see it's a small car with two men inside. They stop and ask you if you need a ride. You say no, not sure if that's the best choice, but with Doña Estela's words about men, you don't want to chance it. Dawn will break soon and you'll be able to see where you're going, maybe catch a bus back to Paracho and find your band. It's a small enough place and someone will know where they are. The car drives off and you continue, your mind swirling about. Now you hear an engine behind you. You turn around to see the high beams of a wide vehicle approaching. Damn! If that's Fedi being a smart-ass, you're going to have to punch him once and for all. The lights dizzy you. A silhouetted figure approaches. It doesn't seem to be any of the guys. Pato is too big, Charlie walks like a gringo and Fedi walks like he's just won a soccer game. Maybe they found a mechanic. That damn light is so freakishly bright! The next thing you know, you see black on the edges of your vision growing larger and closing in until no white remains. You fall to the ground.

Turn to page 40.

NARCOLANDIA
(continued from "Walking")

You wake up in blackness. The Tarahumara doll pokes into your behind as the floor you're sitting on hums and vibrates. You must be traveling in some vehicle. There's a cloth in your dry mouth. You can't swallow. You can only make whimpering noises, not the kind of noises *you* wanna make, but it's all you can muster when you realize your hands are tied up behind you. *Shit!* You feel a pressure around your head. You must be blindfolded. You try separating your hands, but the restraints tighten. You try to separate your ankles and they move with ease. After a bit of wrangling, you wrench them free! Bit by bit you curl your legs cross-legged then push up toward a standing position until you bang your head against a low ceiling. You hear snickering. You're not alone.

"Look, the roquera woke up!" says a youngish sounding man. He's no one you know. "You think you got street cred. You wanted to knife us, huh? The only knifing is gonna be from us, you understand?"

"Ah," says a raspy voice, "At last. My companion may be a bit impulsive. Don't worry. Nothing much will happen to you if you *behave.* You can start by answering our questions. Where are you from?" You find yourself answering honestly.

"El D.F."

"A runaway," mumbles the younger one.

"Perhaps not," says Raspy Voice Man. "Who are your parents and why do they let you wander about these wild lands unsupervised?" he continues. You tell them their names. *Damn it!*

"The wrong one. Didn't I tell you, Jefe?" the younger one exclaims.

"Shut up! I don't want any of your lip! You're just a foot soldier or better said, a punk-ass kid. You're replaceable, remember?"

Foot Soldier continues as if nothing negative were said. "What are we going to do?"

"We're going to have to wait for el Capo."

"Maybe we should let her play that piece of junk instrument to pass the time."

"No. Don't give her anything!"

It's getting hotter and hotter in the back of the truck or RV or whatever you're in. No A.C. for you, or for Foot Soldier or this raspy voiced man. Neither of them can be *that* important. Whoever they are, at least they don't touch you...not yet. This is kind of surprising. Why haven't they touched you? They could have gotten away with it. You've been kidnapped. Rape is the logical next step before they dismember and murder you. Your stomach tightens. Nobody in your life knows where you are and these guys don't see you as human. It's almost like you don't exist already. It's like you got swallowed up by a giant beast leaving no trail, no remains, no whisper of your life.

At last, your kidnappers start chattering. The eavesdropping helps you feel alive. They sound like the top-50 music stations with all this celebrity gossip, but you prefer that to their talks about guns and ammo. When it's time to eat some roadside food, one of the guys pounds on solid metal, then you hear the sound of a roll up door like on a small moving truck. It's always that door, every time they stop. One of them stays with you while the other goes out to get nourishment. The two of them never talk about the plans or the people from their organization, not even somebody boning so-and-so's wife, nothing that would give you a clue as to what kind of people these are exactly. You retreat to the depths of your mind, replaying music, all the parts: the bass, the guitar, the violin and drum. Time means nothing. Meal breaks are the only events that give you a sense of time, but even those are not regular. When Foot Soldier ungags you, the truck is already rolling, of course. You know the routine by now: no biting, no screaming. You're on the highway; no one can hear you anyhow. They have given you juice and water here and there. They want you alive, at least for now. This time, Foot Soldier puts his fingers deep into your mouth. You retch. You're about to bite him when you taste carnitas. Oh, yeah. Thereafter he feeds you less clumsily; more food and less fingers. You feel like a food-crazed animal. Eating feels like vicious sex. Like when you know you're supposed to slow down…you know you're not supposed to like it like that…but all you want is more, anyway you can get it. You'll take it clumsy. You'll take it when it hurts.

You can only assume you're going north. Most of these narco thugs do business in northern México, including the southwestern United States. Then something strange occurs: Foot Soldier actually *talks* to you. Just a few words. But you're amazed after so much deprivation. "Hey, bet you wish you weren't tied up in this truck, huh?"

You don't answer. You want to say something sassy, but your voice isn't used to sounding. The muscle movements involved for talking are foreign to you. You manage a sort of moan.

"If you could do anything, what would you be doing right now?"

"Huh?"

"You know, like if you were free to do as you wanted…"

"Instead of tied up in this truck?" The words come out slow and intentional.

"Yeah."

"Play my stand up bass at the top of El Templo del Sol. That's what I'd do."

"You're a serious musician, eh? Me, too." You say nothing. This whole situation is so strange. Is he supposed to be a pal now? "I play guitar, too."

"What kind?" Your curiosity makes you speak.

"Classical when I'm alone, but mainly I play in a Norteño group and a few wedding gigs here and there."

The truck stops again. Foot Soldier leaves you in the truck. You can tell by the warm breeze on your cheeks that the rollup door is open. You hear conversations outside and a new voice. El Capo is here. His voice pierces like a crystal spear. He's the boss. You can't tell what region or even what country he is from. His Spanish is textbook perfect. Wow, it's as if he chooses his words with freaky precision, not an extra word, not one! Yet what he is saying is not canned. You can tell he is in the moment, thinking, planning.

Now Raspy Voice guy is asking whether the capo will take you, sexually. You notice that instead of holding you, Foot Soldier is rummaging through some bags. You want to make a run for it, but you're still fucking blindfolded.

This is a dead end.

Turn back to an earlier page and choose another path.

"Your silence will not protect you."

Audre Lorde

ON THE ROAD ONCE AGAIN

(continued from "Quinceañera")

Your head hurts the next day, especially your eyes and the back of your neck. It's hard to hear Fedi go on about how many autographs he signed. Apparently it's pretty well known he played for Bang Data last spring.

"What's-a-matter, Chela, you're so sad you make an onion cry!"

Everyone chortles. You just look out at the road. As you head north along the 15 toll-road, a sense of dread infiltrates your blood-stream like a too-strong live-vaccine someone pricked you with when you were sleeping. It's in you now. You don't know what to make of the rumors and headlines. The gist: northern México has become like Chicago of the 1930s or more like Medellín of the 1980s. The cartels rule. They've taken over local governments and sections of the Mexican military. Rumors say even federal agencies from the United States have succumbed. Maybe worse, their bullying and fear tactics have people bending to accommodate their violent whims like trees in a hurricane. You're about to enter the territory of the Sinaloa Cartel. The plan is to keep driving *past* the greater Culiacán area. The toll roads should be safe and although your vehicle stands out—with the Los Huérfanos del D.F. logo spray painted on the doors—it's obvious you're from the south, but at least it doesn't look like you have any money. The sign reads: 16 Kilometers to Culiacán. You're glad this highway skirts *around* the city and is monitored by Los Federales. They should stave off any narco violence as long as you stay on the freeway. Then again, what about Los Zeta. They worked for the federal government and then went rogue and allied themselves first with the Gulf Cartel, then the Beltrán Leyva Cartel and now are vying to snatch this territory from the Sinaloans. You're in the cartel border-lands, which is the worst place you could be in. Your mind starts running circles around everything you know about the cartels…the gruesome pictures in the nota roja magazine, ¡*Alarma!*…the freaky videos on YouTube of beheadings and rapes. You glance at the gas gauge, three quarters full. Thank God! By now you're at the outskirts just west of Culiacán. Pato's voice startles you. "Hey, Chela."

"Yeah?"

"I need to eat, *now!*" Nausea shoots through you. *Could he have any worse timing?* Your fists grip the steering wheel. Pato is a diabetic; his food needs are real and Pato is the best friend you have.

"OK, OK. We'll pull over. I promise."

You find your fingers turning pale. The doctor said you got to take better care of your hands. No fighting. No heavy lifting. Not good for your dexterity, not at all. You take a deep breath and force yourself to turn off the highway. Before you know it you've entered El Ejido San Jose de Guanajuato, Culiacán's half-assed suburb. Tacos, tacos, everyone eats tacos in northern México. There's gotta be a quick place to eat.

"To the left! To the left!" Charlie hollers. Too late. You're forced to go around the block. The next thing you know, you find yourself stuck in gridlock traffic. What's going on? To your left you see a trian-gular modern cathedral flanked by fifty Carmelita nuns chanting and holding up signs. Nuns are your least favorite people.

You flash to her aunt, Arcadia's, the one with all the family money. She had been a nun and took a vow of poverty, but no one seemed to mind when she funded local schools, universities and possibly some politicians' campaigns on the side. You remember her face half-covered by the habit. You wanted to scream out, "Show yourself! Don't be hiding in the light!" (A biblical reference you learned from watching the X-Files with your mom.)

"Fuuuuuuuck!!!!" you scream.

"Hey, Chela, get a hold of yourself!" Fedi says.

"What are all these nuns doing here?" You see pairs of nuns holding up large hand-painted banners with life-sized portraits of big-eyed saints and other important people. The banners are supported by sapling trunks stripped of their bark. You take note of some signs: La Historia No Te Obsolverá, Deuteronomio 5:17 No Matarás and No Te Olvides de Sor Juana Castellano-Jimenez.

"Check it out, Chela. They're having some kind of demonstration. Look at those signs. Damn, they must be heavy! What's up with the martyred saints?" Pato tries to distract you. Only he knows the *real* story about how you started hating nuns. It wasn't until you were seventeen that it all went down so badly for you.

Charlie interjects, "Yo, most saints were martyred…that's kind of the point…dying for Christianity. What's up with that? I don't think anyone is going to canonize me if I die for music!"

"You'd have to wait in line after Tupac and a whole bunch of them gangsta cabrones…" Pato starts.

"Eh! Don't talk about what you don't understand." Fedi insists. "These are not just martyred saints, if you guys knew anything…."

You tune him out. Your eyes go back to the sign about Sor Juana whatever-her-name is. *Ugh. Why that name? Why not Sor María or something?* This you say to yourself.

Flash to the portrait of Sor Juana Inez de la Cruz in the Chancellor's office at El Conservatorio Internacional de Música. There she looked down on you with her plain pious face. Even that was a lie…she was supposed to be quite a looker before she committed herself to God.

You catch the tail end of Fedi's soliloquy. "These are *beheaded* saints. Look, there's St. John the Baptist, St. Dennis, St. Gregory and many I've never heard of like John of Senhout. Hey, but look there's our fathers of the Revolution Miguel Hidalgo and Ignacio Allende. Look there's Apostle Paul!"

"This is sick!" you mumble. You never got how Fedi believes God saved him from being another street-side casualty when he was drug-running back in the hood. He *chose* to leave that life behind!

Pato thought you were sick for changing in your two hundred peso bills, the ones sporting the portrait of México's famous scholar, Sor Juana Inez de la Cruz. "Don't you wanna see your sister being represented, huh comadre?" Yes. Her poetry helped people imagine México as more than just a colony, but a nation of its own, one with ideas. She was supposed to be some kind of genius reading at age three. Daughter of a single mom, but of pure Spanish pedigree. She, like Chavela Vargas, wrote love poetry to women. Who were these women she loved so? You try to imagine life locked up in the convent devoted to God and literature and helping the needy cut by this thread of guilt and shame for her desires. She must have punished herself for her eccentricities at the beginning. Sor Juana could have been a hero to you…at least for her daring, fuck-what-they-think attitude until she ruined it.

Pato pulls you by the hand. "I need to eat *now*!"

"Right, right." You scan around and see a taco truck across from the cathedral. Against your mother's advice, you abandon the car right there. Traffic isn't really moving anyhow. A large crowd of spectators fills up the street. You all head over to the tacos, keeping an eye on the car. There are workers lounging around a gaping trench along the sidewalk. Brown, cloudy water pools there. Tacos and tortas rest in the mitt-like hands of the workers. Nobody eats. Nobody works. Everyone stares ahead at the nuns. A fugue of whispers haunts the ear-space, until Pato tears through the conformity.

"Oiga. Una torta de lengua con aguacate por favor." He orders a tongue and avocado sandwich. The cashier snaps out of the haze and yells out his order to the cook. The sandwich is passing through hands and being assembled. You notice Fedi talking with some older ladies in patent leather shoes and dainty patent leather belts where their waists once were. Charlie steps in to order two platefuls of carnitas tacos.

Back at the car everyone eats, everyone, but you. You sink your head into your hands.

Flash back to the Chancellor's stern looks. The shame on your mother's face. That pinche portrait above you of Sor Juana sitting at a desk surrounded by hand-made books. The burning in your stomach. The bitterness. The betrayal. How could this be happening to you? This you questioned again and again like thudding your fists against a giant colonial wooden door. You were the youngest musician ever admitted there! And because her family regularly gave money to the Conservatorio you had to leave. She wasn't even that talented at flute and she only played one instrument while you played seven! When you left the Chancellor's office you floated down what seemed like the longest hallway ever. Your body was heavy like hunks of wet clay, but your mind floated above, watching. Your mom opened the door to the outside. Light flooded in. You found yourself squinting and then you saw her hiding in the car with her pinche Carmelita aunt. She wanted to confirm your expulsion. See it with her own eyes…and Arcadia was such a coward. She sank into the dark folds of her aunt's habit.

Wake up, Chela. I've got all the dirt. Fedi goes on about how Sister Juana Castellano-Jimenez of the Cross gave refuge to a woman who had been a girlfriend or more like second ho, to this guy on the make from the Sinaloa drug cartel. He goes into too much detail about all the twisted ways they hurt her. You think he exaggerates some parts of it just for the sick pleasure of telling you and watching you squirm. Sister Juana held a town meeting encouraging the people to cleanse the temple of these corrupt businessmen, if you want to call them that. Their words echo some biblical story, of course. But the people were too afraid. Then he goes on about all the atrocities committed by the cartel. Your mind is long gone looping around in fear and then you drift back into the past.

You remember Arcadia's red and puffy eyes that seemed so big on her petite ballerina-like face. Did the fear elevate her eyebrows, making her eyes giant-sized? You remember telling her not to be afraid…that the two of you could shrug this thing off your shoulders together. You wanted her to believe that the bolder she'd dare to stand, the more easily her family would accept it. You asked her to promise to tell them the truth, otherwise you'd take the fall and everyone would think you're some kind of pervert, forcing yourself on her instead of a mutually consenting relationship. She didn't promise. She just stared at you for hours until the sun came out. Then, without a word, she ran out the door.

All the Carmelita nuns have left of their departed sister Sor Juana is her head. The girl was never found and the town surrounding the nunnery, silent. No witnesses. Nobody knows anything. People are afraid to gossip in case the conversation spreads out into heavily mined territory. Folks keep to themselves these days. No one sings as they work. No one whistles while strolling around the Plaza de Armas. The life and breath of the town is gone. Not even the wind blows there.

The birds have gone, leaving mosquitoes to rule the evenings. People stay indoors after 4 p.m. The quiet before the storm lingers.

So the nuns made a pilgrimage to El Templo del Carmen, in Ejido San Jose de Guanajuato outside of Culiacán proper, to conjure back the wind. They came to sit, to chant, to sing, to yell about all this injustice when nobody else would speak of it.

Fedi, who is usually all about himself, wants to stay and support the nuns. He's getting into all this liberation theology ranting. He thinks the nuns should go all-out and make signs saying, "Go Ahead, Make Me A Martyr, Too!"

"You want to be a martyr for these nuns, Fedi?" Pato looks at him ferociously.

"Open your fucking eyes, man, this isn't about a bunch of nuns, or for a missing woman. This is for all of México. El pueblo unido. Someone needs to take these guys down!"

"Whoa, whoa Fedi, you're my carnal, but I ain't going out like that!" Charlie pipes up. "I'm down for the pueblo, but I'm not feeling you here. We are way over our heads with this. Over forty thousand people have died for this drug war business. This is too fucking big!"

"That's what they said to David and he took down Goliath. Come on, Charlie, you must know about this…you're Jewish." You can't hold back any longer.

"You wanna stay here, Fedi? You're a fly in their eyes. They will kill you in a hot second!"

"You're a chicken-shit, Chela. You're a coward with this, just like you're a coward with your personal life, and *you know* what I'm talking about! These parasites thrive on people like you. I'm telling you if people would rise together…ah, forget it. You don't understand because you've had this sheltered life. No one was there to protect *me*. No one. I had to find my own way out of the streets!"

With that, Fedi dives into the crowd of black and white frocks, the crowd of signs with saints painted on them, saints with very large eyes. He picks up a "Thou shalt not kill sign." He stands out with his hand-screened blood colored Bang Data tee as the only non-clergy person actively protesting. Very few priests have joined the group for that matter. At this rate, you'll never get to L.A. on time! His words fester in your mind. Coward. Coward. Coward! Why didn't you say anything when the Chancellor asked you? Your silence made it seem like you forced yourself on her! Your silence got you kicked out of school. You kept hoping someone would stand up for you and it pissed you off that no one did. Arcadia got respect. Arcadia was believed. Arcadia's father's side of the family is pure Spanish, somehow descended from the 10th Muse of the World, Sor Juan Inés de la Cruz, that brilliant bad-assed nun who wrote about love for women and women's right to vote before she too cowered under the Inquisition and stopped writing. They got to her. They scared her into silence. But then again, who dared to stand up for her in the pinche Seventeenth century? Probably no one! Only three hundred fifty years later do they have the guts to put her on the 200-peso bill. That's a long time to lay low in guilt and fear…a long time for almost no one to have her back.

Turn to page 51.

EL PUEBLO UNIDO

(continued from "On The Road Once Again")

"**L**ook," you insist. "Fedi has lost his fucking mind! We've gotta get outta here!" You rush over to the wagon, keys in hand. You're surprised to see Charlie run after you.

"Chela, this is some messed up shit!"

"Messed up? It's Fedi with his diva melodramatics off to save these nuns or so he says! I say fuck him. He can stay here. We need to go on with this tour, now!"

"Yo, Chela, I feel you. Fedi is tripping big-time, but we have to support him. He needs our help."

"Do you really think he would do the same for us?"

"Hard to say, but think about it: we can't go on tour without him. He's our lead guitar player. For many of our fans, he's the face of the band cuz he's the one with the most fame now."

Now you feel like an idiot for making up this whole tour pretense. That's just the cover story to get your hands on the Perfumed Lady before that jerk American dude dumps her in the garbage or sells her off. You sigh.

"OK, Charlie. Let's convince him to leave…but that's gonna be hard considering how freakishly stubborn he is"

"True that sister. True that!"

So the religious community of El Ejido San Jose de Guanajuato halfheartedly welcomes you. You end up staying at their lodgings just out of town. The local monastery moved in to attempt to protect the nuns. The dormitories are separated by gender so you end up away from your buddies at night. All alone, except for the nuns, but they don't count as company to you. Pato uses his brawn and creativity to create more signs, Charlie and you end up stuck on the letter-writing campaign thanks to your superior literary skills, and Fedi hijacks an ice cream truck to circle about the El Ejido San Jose de Guanajuato with the loudest megaphone screaming out slogans and demanding justice. He starts off focusing on the issues at hand. To the thugs, he insists the killings stop and to the community, he demands that people speak up and rise up against the cartel. At dinner, you notice after his first day of ice cream truck rantings, a few nuns flock to him. You're in a mega-sized dining hall with the women designated to sit on one side and the men on the other. Three nuns usher Fedi to sit at the border between the allotted genders, that way they can chat with him while they eat. You overhear bits of their conversation. Seems like the nuns see Fedi as some kind of junior savior, a gem in ragamuffin clothing.

The next day at lunch, Fedi starts implying you're all cowards for not going on the frontlines like him.

"Look," says Pato. "You've got to stop this shit. We're backing you up doing all this media work. Don't you think Jesus would understand that not everybody has this kind of frontlines activism style? I mean, there's a place for other kinds of righteous work, isn't there?"

Fedi doesn't say a thing. He just grips his fork like he's strangling it.

By the third day, you think Fedi has seriously lost it. Some of his one-liners hit below the belt and border on homophobic, implying that the cartel leaders were all screwing each other and making themselves stupid with sex. "You're going to get sloppy, you motherfuckers, and then retribution will be yours, Holy and otherwise."

At dinner you expect the nuns to stay away from him now that he's crossed a line sounding like the ghetto warrior he tries not to be. But no, now the fifteen nuns or so have thrown aside the whole segregated gender thing. They are eating on the men's side. No one says anything about it, not even the Superiors. Everyone knows these are trying times. Some believe they are being tested by God to cast traditions and regulations to the side and find new ways of doing God's work. The end result: some of these nuns are eating out of Fedi's hands. It even looks like they are flirting with him...if that's not a sin to ponder. You watch him. He seems better-spoken and more mature. From the little you do overhear, he's actually not cussing. He's not spitting loogies on the ground. He's not wiping his moco-face with his sleeve, but rather using a handkerchief!

Fedi never walks alone. They're always watching all of you and nearly touching him. Nuns guide him around the place with its maze-like inner hallways and colonnades. You barely speak to Fedi. You'd have to wade through the robes to get to him and you don't have the patience or the social skills. You've got to find a way to get out of there and fast! You're already likely to miss your first gig. There's still time to get the Perfumed Lady if you leave the day after tomorrow at the latest. Then everything else would have to slip into place without a hitch. Unlikely. You find your heart racing at random moments throughout the day. One of the nuns hooks you up with some anointing wine, lots of it. It's the only thing that keeps you from throwing yourself up against a stone pillar. One time, when you're taking a break near a little fountain, you notice this fresco of a thorny Jesus on the wall opposite the colonnade. You stare at it. Why do Latin Americans have to have the bloodiest Jesuses, who knows? You look at his large tearful eyes, his resignation to suffering. Fuck it! You don't want to suffer! You don't want to look back at these days wondering why you catered to Fedi, yet again! You just want to snatch the barbed vines from Jesus' head and coil them around Fedi's little neck and pull hard! When you catch Fedi talking to only one robe, you break forth, practically pushing the Nun to the side.

"Fedi, I've had it up to here with all this!"

"What? Excuse me, Sister."

"Pato and I are heading a freakin' international human rights campaign. We're in touch with every organization that will listen to us and every reporter that gives a damn. I've licked so many envelopes and so many of these old-fashioned stamps my tongue is turning to mush, not to mention I must be on ten thousand hit lists what with these cartel bullies and all the negative virtual press they're getting now. Do you know how hard it is to bring attention to these issues without glorifying these jerks or running some sort of shock value campaign with the way they've been mutilating so many people? It's unreal, man, and reporting the truth is fucking garish! And meanwhile, *where the hell are you?* Talking the big talk in some ice cream truck? If that's even what you're doing!"

Time slows down. You see Fedi's face redden and that vein in his forehead pop out. He takes a deep breath while lifting up his arm. He's about to lose it in front of a Superior nun. This could be the moment you've been waiting for!

"I agree with you, young lady." You turn and look at the nun wide eyed. "With your last point in particular. We don't know where Fedi goes in that truck. No one does."

"Evasive Maneuvers, Mother Superior." Fedi pipes up. "I keep changing my route so they'll be less likely to corner me somewhere. I take measures to stash the truck. I've got a couple of sweet hiding places. That way just when they think they've got me, I'll set off on foot. So far they don't know what I look like, do they?"

"Let's thank the Lord you've managed so well so far, my son!" She pauses and genuflects. You want to puke! "But I'm worried, my son. If none of us know your route then in case—and God forbid this should happen, but we must be prudent and prepare for the worst while praying for the best—in case something were to happen to you, we would not know where to look. We would not be able to provide medical attention in a timely manner, if it were needed."

Fedi appears like a young boy asking his grandmother for advice, "What do you think I should do?"

———————

Turn to page 55.

ICE CREAM TRUCK
(continued from "El Pueblo Unido")

"**F**ederico, I think you should sketch out a map of where you're planning to go more or less each day. Give the sketch to me and me alone. Then make sure to call us every hour on the hour so we know you're all right. That way, if you fail to call, we will know where to go searching for you." Her eyes are big and commanding. "Now, it's not up to me to judge the content of another's soul, but these sorts of fellows, well, words can't describe the means to which they are willing to avail themselves. Time and God's Will, along with our coordination may be the only things to save you if, God forbid, they were to apprehend you for the purpose of their evils."

Fedi looks shaken. You wonder if he hadn't even considered he may actually get nabbed by these bastards. Did he think his fame and pretty face would protect him? Your mind drifts to all of those gorgeous women who got nabbed coming home from work in the dark from the Maquiladoras on the outskirts of Ciudad Juárez.

"All right, all right, Mother Superior. Have you got a pencil?" You walk away as he scrawls out something. The scratching of the pencil echoes against the surrounding stone bodies.

When Fedi comes home that evening he seems as confident

as ever. But you wonder if her words are eating fear into him. He does respect her. Apparently, he managed to call every hour like he promised and Fedi was never one to be punctual. The next day, he doesn't call at three pm and by 3:05, you're on duty as part of the search party. You ride into town along with Pato and two wide-shouldered nuns in a royal blue minivan with white lettering announcing parochial allegiances. *Great, way to lay low!* At 2:45 he was supposed to stash the truck in hiding place number two, behind the foliage of this giant puffball of a tree. From the street, you can barely tell if it's there. The black tires are so thoroughly shaded and the rest covered by foliage. You all approach with quiet steps. You duck under the lowest branches. There are shell casings at your feet. You freeze. Pato is standing two meters behind you. You cast your eyes over to the visible parts of the truck and those are full of holes. One of the nuns steps forward and runs her hand along the broken surface of the truck. She turns her head toward you. "I will go inside if you like, sister."

Your knees wobble and you hold them with your hands. You hear Pato gasping right behind you.

If you choose to let the sister check the inside of the ice cream truck, turn to page 57.

If you choose to step up and check it yourself, turn to page 58.

THE NUN STEPS UP

(continued from "Ice Cream Truck")

"Thank you sister." You reach for Pato's hand and clamp down on it. His body sways like his middle were made of jelly. You start looking at the worn spots in your boots.

"Good news. There's no body and there's no blood. We should look for a ransom note, but so far it would appear that God has more plans for your friend Federico here on earth."

You triple the search party to scope out different parts of town simultaneously. The local police make gestures as if they're helping search for their pseudo-celebrity out-of-towner. Fedi has become quite famous by now, the face behind the outrage and all that. After a long day of hitting the pavement, you return to the religious campus in silence. You lie in your bed of stiff wool blankets and cotton sheets, face down in a rather fibrous pillow. You fall asleep with the light on. Later you hear a click and you're in total darkness. You hear a whisper, "Chela..." Your heart shoots out of the gate like a racehorse.

Turn to page 59.

YOU STEP UP
(continued from "Ice Cream Truck")

"**N**o thank you, sister. I think I should go in. I owe it to him in a way." You won't be a coward this time! You take a deep breath and step to the door. It's completely closed, which seems odd. You think it would hang open like a tired tongue what with all those bullet holes. You grip the turn handle and rotate it down until it clicks. The sonic blast of white heat is the last thing you sense.

This is a dead end.
Turn back to an earlier page and choose another path.

A WHISPER IN THE DARK

(continued from "The Nun Steps Up")

"It's me, Charlie."

"Charlie?"

"Yeah. We're getting the fuck out of here, Chela! That's what you wanted, isn't it?"

"Sure, but not like this! I mean, not with Fedi missing. I guess I didn't mean it when I said I wanted to leave his ass behind. I was just…"

"Don't worry about it, Chela. Fedi is already waiting in the back of the wagon. Come on, get your things!"

You get up and pack up by flashlight and creep with him over to the next campus where your station wagon had been stashed. Pato drives, slow and easy, out toward the main road. You hope no one will be manning the gate.

Turn to page 60.

LA CANTINA
(continued from "A Whisper In The Dark")

There is a guard at the gate what with all the recent commotion. The religious community is fearing a widespread violent attack upon the campus itself. Pato pulls up to the gate. Fedi is stashed in the back with the equipment under blankets. Pato throws on the charm while still appearing worried and concerned. You always thought he'd be an amazing actor and you told him so a few times, but he would repeat the same tired old lines about not being skinny enough and not looking European enough. He didn't want to be a "character actor," he wanted to be the main guy. Pato spins a tale to the guard about how the communion wine don't cut it and how ya'll will be drowning your sorrows in a cantina and could he recommend one?

You drive away at a respectful pace. None of you say a word until the next toll stop. You pay without incident, but you notice a bunch of flashlights and a campfire down to the right. "Look," you say to Pato. What's up with that?"

"I don't know. It looks like a camp."

"Why would they camp out here in the middle of nowhere?"

"Maybe it's not nowhere to them."

After about forty minutes of driving, you hear a clunking sound behind you. Fedi emerges and embraces Charlie in the back seat. You can't tell if they're laughing or whimpering. You decided it doesn't really matter. At last, Pato speaks. "So, Fedi, tell Chela and Charlie what happened, but first, put on your pinche seatbelt, man. I don't want to lose you twice!"

"Well, thanks to Saint Michael, I'm here before you now!"

"What are you talking about, Fedi?" You're not getting how learned he has become about all these saint things.

"Seriously. OK, I have a confession. After all the things the Mother Superior said, I started worrying about them coming to get me."

"Well, yeah. You should have been worried four days ago!"

"Shut up, Chela, let me tell the story!"

"Dang, Chela," Charlie starts in. You notice he gets all talking like he's down with it especially when Fedi's around. "Let the brother speak!"

"Anyways, like I was saying, the stress was getting to me. I felt all shaky inside. At lunch, I got some tequila to fill up my hipflask and well, after I stashed the ice cream truck behind the tree, I took a leak right there under the tree and while I did, I said a prayer to St. Michael to protect me."

"Oh, my God, you're like a dog marking his spiritual territory!"

"Shut up Chela. Jesus!"

"So then I ran off real quick. I was like an ocelotl in the jungle after his prey."

"Did you sense they were after you?"

"No, cuz I seriously needed smokes, dude!" He starts to smirk. "Well, I guess they didn't see me run off. *That* was the miracle. I heard the shooting from the little store I was at and I was like I gotta lay low. So I faked like I was hella sick and getting some sort of crazy migraine—my mom used to get those en paz descance—and needed to kick it in their storage room. I promised they could check my pockets when I left and I was making eyes with their daughter and they let me kick it there until nightfall. Then I fucking walked. I walked the fifteen kilometers to the religious compound."

"It's more like ten."

"Shut up, Chela, Dang!" Charlie is livid.

"I don't care, man, let Chela do her Chela thing! So then I crept around the whole darn place, jumped the stone wall and landed on some Mother Superior's mausoleum. It was the freakin' nun cemetery. Yo, I was like praying for forgiveness."

"You know we did go out looking for you for hours, man. Not Charlie. He was stuck using his English skills, but Pato and I and some nuns went over to your hiding spot and saw the truck and…"

"How bad was it, Chela?"

"It was like totally fucked. We were choking up thinking you were dead!" Pato interrupts.

"You were?"

"Even Chela was!" Pato interjects.

"For realz?" Fedi is jumpy.

Charlie leans in and puts his arm around Fedi. It seems to soothe him.

"You bet I was, Fedi. We may not see eye to eye, but I care about you, man. I guess I didn't even realize how much till I thought you might be gone or worse…being tortured. I mean, those guys are really sick…the things they do…"

"I don't want to think about it no more! I accomplished what I set out to accomplish. The nuns got international attention. Let the Red Crosses or Amnistía Mundial handle it now. I served God in my way. I know he didn't want me to go out like that, right there in the ice cream truck. That's why he sent Saint Michael to watch over me! That's why he gathered all those nuns to have my back, just like I had theirs…"

"What! You are trippin', Fedi. Those nuns ratted you out!"

"Don't even say that, Chela! No one ratted me out and especially not Mother Superior. It was just a matter of time like she said that they would find me. El Ejido San Jose de Guanajuato is not that big of a place."

"I hate to say it, man, I bet a lot of those nuns did have your back. They adored you. I could see that. You really meant something to them. But *she* ratted you out. I'm sure of it!"

"Yo, you're paranoid, Chela, especially about *nuns.*"

"What do you know about it Fedi?"

"I don't know the whole story, but I heard about some of your business, OK? Look, I don't want to talk about it anymore. Let's get some grub! I'm seriously hungry after that long walk…however long it was. It was longer than any of you all walked."

You pull over at Angostura and grub at a bar that features carne asada and other beef delicacies along with every kind of hard liquor a proof-drinker would want. You all eat and drink like it's the end of the month with no paycheck coming along. Considering that those cartel guys could be coming after you and your very distinctive station wagon, there actually may be no tomorrow to wake up to.

Turn to page 64.

CHOP SHOP BLUES

(continued from "La Cantina")

You and Pato take driving shifts throughout the night. Someone's snoring really loud in the back. Pato hooks up the MP3 player and busts out with some cool Jazz, keeping it at a low volume.

"Hey, Pato, turn it up. I don't want to fall asleep at the wheel."

"Nah, I'm trying to get a certain effect here."

"What?"

"I need to tell you something, but I don't want the boys to hear."

"How do you know they can't hear us now?"

He calls out, "Fedi and Charlie are cocksucking pussies!" Neither one of them stirs.

"Hey, man, don't dis on the gays, Pato. Not even to prove a point or whatever. My uncle is gay and I have mad love for him and his friends are hella cool."

Pato sighs, "Alright, you got me. I fucked up. I give props to your uncle. He had to escape some scary ass haters. Anyway, I was just messing around."

"Well then, don't say shit like that. If you're gonna be honorable to your word like you say you are then don't spew out those hating side comments even to prove a point to those babies!"

"That's the problem." He lowers his voice, then he lowers his head. "I'm not so honorable as you think I am."

"What do you mean?" You hiss.

"I don't want the guys to know this, but I don't have a fucking visa, Chela."

"Huh? Why not? You have a passport."

"I do have one, that's true but, Chela, it's expired. I got my friend Jimi to forge the dates. Looks pretty good, huh?" He flashes the passport in front of your face.

"I can't look at that while I'm driving. If it looks so good, then why didn't you get a visa when you took Fedi over there. I mean, we had connections there, a que sí?"

"It looks good enough for Los Federales and probably good enough for the border pigs, but not the immigration office. Doesn't matter how many heads your uncle has stroked."

"Shut up, Pato! *Probably* good enough for the border pigs. We're fucked. I can't believe this! You asshole! You're putting us all at risk!"

"Am I, Chela? Am I? Look, I wanted you to get a shot at your dream. I believe in repatriation of sacred objects and body parts for indigenous peoples, so why not instruments? Let's get it out of gringo hands and into ours!"

This is crazy. You can't believe he's willing to risk going to a federal prison just for you. Your throat chokes up. You never told him you had other options like to be a personal assistant for Javier. He busts out into snippets of this Calle 13 song,

"...Por ti, cruzo las fronteras sin visa
Y le saco una buena sonrisa a la Mona Lisa
Por ti, todo lo que hago lo hago por ti
Es que tú me sacas lo mejor de mí
Soy todo lo que soy
Porque tú eres todo lo que quiero..."

that's all about all the risks this guy would take for the person he loves including crossing the border without a visa.

"Sorry, Pato...for saying those things."

"No worries. You're my carnala. I love you, man." And that's all you say to each other until Pato takes the wheel right before dawn.

You arrive at Guaymas in the morning. You feel thrashed, hungover on information. Fedi and Charlie have no hint of Pato's secret. They slept in clueless beauty. Being on the coast and having some tourist appeal makes Guaymas the safest place you've been in a while. Still, your joyfully obnoxious Los Huérfanos del D.F. logo on both sides of the station wagon makes you stand out to random passersby way down the street, let alone someone who could be looking for you. You're about a day's drive to Tijuana and three hours to Nogales, but you don't have to make that decision yet.

Pato's sixth sense for sniffing out tacos leads you to a working-man's taco truck. You all indulge in shrimp-related foods: tostadas, tacos, taquitos and ceviche. Besides you, only men are eating in front of the truck. Probably no wife at home to cook for them. Pato approaches one of the younger guys and spins some yarn about how you were all in this band Los Huérfanos del D.F. but recently you've found God and don't feel like orphans any more. You want to get a new paint job, quick and easy, before your next concert in Nogales. You find the story to be contradictory. Not Pato's best. Whether the guy buys the story or not doesn't much matter. He says he'll take you all there before he has to go to work. He doesn't know the address or the street by name.

Ironically his name is Jesús. No surprise. Everything seems to be ironic these days. He sits in the front with Pato and takes you on a windy circular route within the city. You're glad you didn't protest when Fedi insisted on hanging a crucifix off of the rearview mirror. This act makes your cover story seem more real. Finally, he tells you to stop in a pseudo-abandoned part of town. He hops out of the van and points to the right. There is an entrance to a garage with blackened windows. Pato and Fedi get out to approach the building while you and Charlie stay inside the car. Charlie's in the driver's seat, key in the ignition, just in case. You look around. Jesús is long gone. The air is damp and warm. The heat is revving up. You feel a pang in your stomach. "Hey Charlie, do you think we oughta go in there and look for them? I mean, who knows what kind of place this is?"

"I know, Chela, they could be getting jacked up right now! All the more reason to have the Subaru ready to roll."

You take a long almost labored breath of dense air. You look at each other and both creep out of the car.

You start off ahead, bent over like you are dodging bullets or something till Charlie kicks you in the butt. "Yo, just walk casually. If they see us crouched down, they're gonna think we have guns or something!" He's right. If they see you and think you're armed, they'll want to shoot first. Hopefully they haven't seen you already, not with eyes or with cameras. You start smiling casually. Maybe that will help. You walk up to the building and reach out your hand to the doorknob but before you're able to pull, the door swings backward knocking you down. Charlie swoops in and stands you up like you were some kind of lightweight prop. This could be it; you could be shot right now for being some kind of shifty outsider. But it's only your buddies.

"What are you guys doing here?" Fedi hisses.

"Hey, man, we were worried about you. We've been waiting forever!" It was refreshing to hear Charlie stand up to Fedi for once.

"Everyone back to the car!" Pato demands. At the car, Pato explains the haps. Painting the doors will take too long and besides, this is a chop shop, not an auto detailing shop. The quickest thing they can do is replace the doors and they happen to have replacements. That's a lucky thing. They're not quite the same color, but they should look cool. They're willing to put on the American license plates that Charlie has. Basically you'll have to take everything out of the car or trust that nothing will get damaged or stolen.

"What are we going to do with the stuff, man?" whines Charlie.

"We're going to make a pile out here in the lot and sit on it. Well, you three are going to sit on it while I go off to get food."

No one argues since Pato is the diabetic of the bunch. Pato takes off right away for the food while the rest of you unload all of your equipment and personal effects grumbling to yourselves. You sit on top of a speaker and look east. Fedi faces west and Charlie faces south. There are hills in the distance. One hundred years ago, so much of this area was just wildlands. It was only recently "settled." You all keep to yourselves watching for upcoming looters. Though it's all punked out with stickers, your equipment is valuable and there's gotta be people out there who know it. It is Fedi who speaks first:

"I wonder what is happening back at El Ejido San Jose de Guanajuato? The nuns...the campaign!"

"I thought you said you did your part! You were like the catalyst or some shit and the rest was up to nature."

"Whatever, Chela. Nothing is that simple. I was still getting over escaping with my life when I said that!" He wipes his nose with his sleeve. "What if the narcos attack them now that I'm gone or what if the campaign falls apart? Those nuns believed in me and I kinda let them down. That Mother Superior, she said some deep stuff to me...."

"The Mother Superior ratted you out!"

"Don't say that, Chela, you don't know if that's true! She's very wise. I mean like she studied a lot, but instead of just memorizing and repeating shit, she understands. She gets it!"

"OK, so she's a smart lady, but what does that have to do with you?"

"She told me that Federico means peaceful ruler. The name belonged to one of the Holy Roman Emperors who dedicated his life to collecting sacred objects for the Church way back in the twelfth century."

"You mean a crusader?" Charlie inquires. "That sounds more like a war maker than a peacemaker, man."

"Look, man, if the crusades didn't happen, the Catholic Church would not have the glory that it has today. Having those pieces of ancient apostles and saints is what brings us closer to God. It's what makes more prayers come true!"

"Yo, Fedi, do you know how many of *my people* were killed in the Crusades?"

"*Your people?*"

"Yeah, that's right, *my people*, Jewish people, Middle Eastern people. Women, children, babies, innocent people, whoever supposedly got in their way were killed, man! Even early Christians from the Holy Land were killed because they were brown and spoke Arabic. No one stopped to ask them which *prophet* they believed in!" You notice Charlie, rearing up making his shoulders look stronger.

"I don't believe that!" Fedi squawks.

"Read up man before you start talking!" You look over your shoulder and see Fedi roll up his sleeves. He takes a deep breath and jumps off the pile.

"Hey Fedi, cool down!" you call out.

"Do you realize, Chela, that Charlie here is calling me ignorant. He's trying to be slick about it, but he is!" At this point, Charlie jumps off the pile, too, and takes two steps toward Fedi.

"Forget it, Fedi. We got a job to do now, we gotta watch this stuff. Remember the tour?"

"I can't forget it, Chela. I'm not going to! He acts like he's my carnal, but now he's calling me ignorant! Didn't you hear him?"

"Think of all the fans. Think of all the albums we're going to sell!"

Before you know it, they both leap onto each other and tumble to the asphalt, fists flying. You run your fingers through your hair and tug. "Stop it, guys! Yo, quit it!" Charlie's on the top now, slamming his fists into Fedi's cheek. Just then, Pato shows up, food bags in hand. He starts kicking at their boots.

"Hey, you wusses, show me some real fighting, why don't you!" You don't get why this works, but it does. "And stand up. Stop acting like punk asses and greet me. I come bearing gifts. Let's see, carnitas for you, lengua for Charlie and same old carne asada for Chela."

You all chow down. Charlie has a busted lip that's swelling and Fedi has another gash on his eyebrow and the side of his face is red and puffy. It could have been a lot worse! Maybe their years of camaraderie took some sting out of their fists, maybe. You hope they can clean up nice before the border crossing. All you need is to look like ruffians or poor chumps that got beat up by their coyotes.

Soon the station wagon is ready with the American license plates and its new faded royal blue doors. Ugh. They are the same color blue as the nun van! They definitely do not match with the sparkly midnight blue of the rest of the vehicle, but there's nothing you can do about that now. You're not from here and more importantly, you're in a hurry. Pato pays and you head back onto the highway. You never want to go back to Guaymas, ever.

"What's up with the A.C.?" Fedi bleats.

"I don't know." says Pato. "It *was* working just fine. I'll open up this window."

"Whoa, the air is so damn hot! This fucking car!"

"Hey, don't dis the Subaru, homes. I donated this car to our band. We could be taking the bus right now. Don't forget that!" Charlie stands his ground.

"You wanna start with me?"

"Ay!" You start in. "Stop it, you guys. You're supposed to be the best of friends n shit. I can't handle seeing you fight. You're acting like little boys at school. Man up and shut up!"

"Whoa, Chela, thems is big words for a little gal like you," says Fedi with his best spaghetti western accent.

"Shut up, Fedi!"

"No, *you* shut up!" You bite your lip. This has got to stop. By now Fedi's face is a little skewed from Charlie's handiwork. Charlie's lips are normally on the full side, but now are giant. The cut doesn't show mostly. He looks like he's wearing lipstick. It's kind of cute in a way. With those pretty pouty lips, Charlie looks like the kind of guy that would hang with Tío Gonzalo.

By four o'clock, you've reached Santa Ana and turn off into town. There are beautiful Moorish style buildings everywhere. It's like half Casa Blanca, half Wild, Wild West. At Santa Ana, the roads split: the 15 is a straight-shot to Nogales while the 2 rambles to Tijuana. You don't know which would be more likely to thwart your whole mission: running into some cartel dudes in northern México or having some freaky misunderstanding with the Migra while you're in Southern Arizona. Arizona won't even let people learn about Mexicans. There's gotta be some serious hatred there. People are reporting any suspicious vehicles, that is, any vehicles with brown people in them. California is way more relaxed, from what you hear. On the other hand, if you take the 15, you could be at the border in an hour. You're kind of excited to see the United States.

———————

If you choose to take the 15 and head off to Nogales,
turn to page 77.

If you choose to take Highway 2 and go to Tijuana,
turn to page 72.

HIGHWAY 2
(continued from "Chop Shop Blues")

"Oh, my God, they're fucking following us!"

"Come on, Fedi, you're getting paranoid." You can't believe it. Doesn't he think the Narcos have bigger fish to fry?

"You know, Chela, I agree with Fedi." Charlie pipes in.

"Wow, this is a momentous occasion!" Pato uses his best voice of superiority here.

"Man, shut up, Pato. This is serious. I really don't think Fedi is being paranoid. Haven't you noticed those black SUVs? There's two of them and they both look practically the same, yo!" You and Pato finally look back. In the distance there is a black SUV, but that doesn't mean you're being followed. During some curvy sections of the highway, the SUV even disappears. Pato starts blasting Bendita Maldición and you get tranced out in their music. The landscape appears increasingly foreign to you with its tumbleweeds and saguaro cacti standing tall like priests. You notice semi-disturbing signs along the highway. The one from Mex-Life Insurance says, "People are dying who weren't dying before. Get Mex-Life. What have you got to lose?" You've been in the heart of drug war territory for the last five days and you've felt close to death a few times. Imagine living out here!

"Look, guys, there it is again!" You look back and the SUV is much closer now. You can make out that it has tinted windows and no visible license plate. Maybe the plate's in the back.

"Pretty thug-like, that's for sure!" Charlie says.

"OK, OK, you got me there." You have to admit it. The vehicle dons a power of menace.

"Look, look! I swear to God, there's the other one!"

"Where?"

"Way back there! By that dark rocky patch."

"Shit, he's right." You see it. You see them both and they look like twins. This is not a good sign.

"Relax, guys, this is a Federal Highway. They can't get us here."

"I don't know about that, Pato." Charlie speaks up. "I've heard that people have gotten popped on federal roads too. It's not just local governments that have been corrupted! I can't believe we're doing all this just to play at The Pulse in L.A."

You and Pato look at each other knowing there is so much more behind your escapade.

"Look guys, I'm worried, OK? It's gonna be dark soon and then we won't be able to tell the black SUVs from any other vehicle. They'll be stealth in the darkness."

What Charlie says is true. How will you know if you're being followed once the darkness hits?

"Hey, I'm sorry, man." Fedi starts. You're surprised. This is not a guy to apologize. "It was me that convinced you to do this tour and you've been hella nice the whole time. You've been a brother to me, man. I've always wanted to play in the US. Always. And I thought I was gonna when I played with Bang Data...but when their guitar player got better, I was off the bill...just like that! I played with them for almost six months. They *acted* like I was family..."

"You were great with them, Fedi. I heard the bootleg recordings. But even with their corporate music contracts and community organizing, they couldn't get the right visa for you. Come on now! If they're deporting students who were practically born there, why would they care about your rascuache ass?"

"I know that, Chela!"

"Fedi, I'm just trying to say you are good enough to play with a band like that and they, they probably..."

"Hey guys, good news. We haven't gotten gunned down yet and

the toll is coming up. If these really are the cartel guys we think they are, they might even get detained at the checkpoint. Wouldn't that be cool?" Pato has a way of making everyone calm in a crisis, as long as he's not in crisis himself. Keeping him well-fed helps. Why not just tattletale on these SUV guys at the next tollbooth? Then the Feds could go after those snakes as long as their bribe wasn't too tempting. Worst-case scenario: Los Federales would assume you were at fault, too, and that could be a whole drama to work out, a drama that could lead to your imprisonment.

At the toll road, someone asks you if you've seen anything suspicious. Here's your chance to tell them about the SUVs. "No, nothing suspicious." Pato interjects. "What should we be looking for, sir?"

"Watch out for hitch-hikers, of course, or any large objects in the road or to the side of the road. Do not pull over unnecessarily. Do not take any side roads or shortcuts. Do not pull over for any sirens or megaphones unless you're sure it's the police or ambulance."

His speech sounds rehearsed. Then he pauses to check some devices he has on his belt. "Oh, excuse me, Mr. Patricio Barraza, I see here you have a lot of metal objects in your vehicle. Can you tell me about that? You don't have an arsenal in there do you?" At that he smiles. But you know it's not that simple.

"No, no, of course not. We're in a rock band and we're going on tour. Some of our equipment comes in metal cases."

"Of course, that makes sense. We're going to have to inspect the vehicle anyway. Sorry for the inconvenience. Please drive up to that yellow line and let our men guide you to the inspection area."

"Yes sir." You do as you are told. The men in brown uniforms lead you to a little side road where you park and are ordered to step out of the vehicle. It's evening now and you grab your jacket for warmth. Of course they have to feel you up to make sure you have no concealed weapons in your jacket. You feel stiff as their hands cascade the sides of your body. Your jeans are fitting tighter and your lonjas popping out the tops of your hip-huggers. You feel a quiver when their hands brush your skin. You try to focus on the guys ripping apart the vehicle. No, for real. They even go into the lining of the car. Sure, the guys put it back in the end, but it's sort of crooked and looks like the station wagon is wearing too big hand-me-down clothes.

The guard from the tollbooth walks over to you. He clearly has rank over the repo men. "It's the CD cases." He says. "The metal ones, they look like weapons cases. So naturally we had to open them. Very fancy."

"Sure sir, no problem."

"Los Huérfanos del D.F. That's the name of your band?"

"Yes sir, it is."

"Federico Martínez. Is that one of your members?" Pato pauses at this question. What is he gonna say? "Well, is he or is he not one of your members? It says so on the CD, the one you're going to try to sell up there in the north, right?"

"Yes, I am one of the members, officer." Fedi steps up to take his fate like a man.

"I thought that was you. Can I trouble you for your autograph? My little nephew is a big fan. You *did* play with Bang Data, right?"

"Yes I did. I did play with Bang Data." While Fedi autographs nearly a dozen CDs for Los Federales, the rest of you repack the equipment and your personal items into the station wagon. As you carry in a monitor, you sort of stumble into Charlie and end up rubbing up against him sideways. His body feels so warm to you in the chill of the desert evening.

During the rest of the ride toward Tijuana, you're silent, sitting up front with Charlie driving. This way you've got your bases covered. Charlie is the American of the group so if they only bother to ask him his citizenship, he can say US and it will be true. You sitting next to him as a female counterpart looks good in their eyes...plus you have a Mexican passport. If only Pato's was up to date! You're still the only one that knows about it. Part of you wants to tell the group so you could better prepare for the potential drama with the border officers. But then you're afraid that they'll wanna cancel the tour and you'll never get the Perfumed Lady. You probably should have gone by yourself.

You look at Charlie's profile while he's driving. He looks different to you somehow. His features appear more chiseled, more adult. His posture more upright, more ready to face the world. He turns over to you. "Ten more kilometers to TJ, I can't believe we're almost there, Chela. We'll have to show our hand at the border and we got no aces up our sleeves."

"We got charm. We got American plates. We got visas. We got passports." Pato calls out from the back. "Let's all stay calm. We can do this! We can!"

———⌒———

Turn to page 79.

NOGALES

(continued from "Chop Shop Blues")

As you head toward Nogales, your gut feels wrong. Maybe it's the heat that makes you feel bloated like road kill. The air conditioning continues to dwindle. Charlie is in the driver's seat in preparation for your eventual border crossing. With him up front you hope to keep peace between Fedi and Charlie. The heat is bad enough. The desert blurs by, but you catch glimpses of saguaros with scarecrow arms stretched out against the sky. The occasional patches of shrubs make you think of oases. But you know there's nothing there. The whole place feels haunted. The red tones in the earth remind you of Mars. Five, six, seven o'clock and you swear it's getting hotter. Your butt sits in a sticky puddle. You hope no one will notice when you stop to pee. They'll be talking about this one for a while. You may even get a nickname out of it like: "Chela of the swamp" or whatever.

Soon you arrive at Cibuta. You see what looks like high valley grazing lands surrounded by bespeckled mountains. The town dons a smattering of dusty run-down buildings. You find a taco truck and pull over. You stay in the car—not wanting anyone to see your damp behind—and have Pato order you the same old, same old: three tacos de carne asada con aguacate y zanahorias picantes. Your bandmates grab their food and join you in the car. After chowing down, Charlie turns the key and pulls out. Before you know it, the town is behind you and Nogales ahead of you. You really don't have much of a plan.

Plan A: Hope they don't stop you. Plan B: Hope the letters from the club owners are enough.

You're feeling drowsy, like you're about to fall asleep. Maybe you could sleep through this whole border ordeal. Maybe if you slept, it would all go away. You take one last look around, at the mountains, the bushes, the skyline and then you notice you're surrounded by black SUVs. "Charlie, look!" You hear the sounds of fast-paced lightning hit the back of the wagon first, getting louder until you feel your body shaking. You've been shot up. You don't want to turn your head to see what went down behind you. The shock doesn't let you feel the pain, at least not yet. You shut your eyes and play Mingus' "Haitian Fight Song" in your head. You go out in music, bold and lively music.

———————

This is a dead end.

Turn back to an earlier page and choose another path

TÍA JUANA

(continued from "Highway 2")

"Whoa, TJ has changed!" Pato exclaims after a long silence. You thought he was sleeping. It's past midnight by now."

"When have *you* been here?" You had never heard any stories of TJ.

"I used to live here with my aunt, but on the west side in Playas de Tijuana."

"Hey, Pato, is it true that there really was a Tía Juana back in the time of Prohibition? I heard this was a cow town back then and this lady, Tía Juana, used to own a cantina with some great grub."

"Nah, Charlie, that's some gringo myth-story. Tijuana is older than that. Some day we'll have to come back, hang with my tía for a couple days and I can show you where all the good eats are and some of the history stuff, too."

"I'm happy to show you around San Diego, when we have more time." Charlie replies.

Pato starts coughing. "I've been there before, but I wouldn't say I *know* it. It's a big place."

"So is TJ now."

"Tijuana has really expanded," Pato goes on. "So many people come here expecting to cross into the Promised Land, but get stuck for one reason or another. I bet some of them wish there was a Tía Juana to take care of them, make it all work out…"

"Yeah, them and the gringos with the worst mezcal hangovers, or the ones who get pickpocketed or lost. They're all looking for Tía like some big-shouldered indigenous wet-nurse..." you add with a snarky tone.

"Tijuan means city by the sea or some shit like that to the original inhabitants. There ain't been no nursemaid Juana." Everyone looks at Fedi. "Hey, yo, I'm up on my indio shit."

"Enough history," starts Pato. "We gotta make a plan. We'll be at the border in like twenty minutes. It's fucking one in the morning. We gotta get into the psyche of these border pigs. Shifts start at midnight, so these guys are fresh considering this is a whacked time to be working for one's what do you call it, uh, circadian rhythms. So they might be more on their game..."

"Don't you think this is like the hoodlum hour? Aren't they expecting bad shit to go down?" Fedi asks.

"Not necessarily. But it's not like we're headed right for Disneylandia. So I guess what I'm saying is we could, I think, stay with my aunt for one night. She does live on the other side of town. It would take forty fives minutes to get there at least. This traffic is insane! Or we could hope that someone's too tired to care..."

"Care about what?" Fedi asks. "We got all our paper squared away thanks to you, man."

"That's true. But they look for excuses. They don't want our kind. We're only halfway middle class here." He turns to look at you. You feel hot air budding in your throat. You expected Pato would have confessed he didn't have a visa instead of shifting the focus to you. This isn't like him. He goes on, "Let me repeat the options. We could cross now, get it over with and hope we get someone on the groggy side or we could come back at rush hour after having four hours of sleep or so and cross then."

"Let's do it now. Let's Charge!" says Fedi.

"I say wait till tomorrow. I think they're more likely to let us through during rush-hour," says Charlie. Disagreeing with Fedi again.

"Hey, guys, let's let the *woman* decide. What does your *natural* intuition tell you, Chela?" Fuck. Your intuition is thrashed. You want to cross the border so badly and hurry so you can get your bass.

Tomorrow by five pm is the last possible day. Your desires clog up your natural flow of intuition. They really do.

If you decide to cross now, turn to page 82.

If you decide to return at rush hour, turn to page 109.

AHORA, SÍ

(continued from "Tía Juana")

"**D**ang, look at all that traffic! Watch out for drunks. This is the party crowd for sure!" Charlie is originally from New York City. His mother is a professor and his father a nurse practitioner in a hospital. They came out west to San Diego when he was fifteen and never left the place. TJ, Rosarito and Ensenada became his stomping grounds.

You're almost at the part where you can't turn around any more, when you catch a glimpse of the border up ahead. There are like twenty tollbooths each with the capacity to weigh and scan the entire vehicle. You wonder if there are special high-powered microphones to pick up people's desperate whispers. You notice all kinds of red flashing lights up ahead. "Guys, look at the lights!"

"Hey," Charlie calls to the guys in the back. "Stick your heads out the windows. Check it out!" As the road curves you see even more flashing lights. It looks like some kind of show for the masses. You freeze for a moment as the lights grow larger and more plentiful. Finally, you speak your mind.

"Charlie, I think we should turn back. Let's cross somewhere else."

"I doubt this whole light thing will even matter, Chela."

———————⌇———————

If you're bent on convincing him to cross somewhere else and avoid the red flashing lights, turn to page 84.

If you go on ahead and cross here and now, turn to page 90.

SOMEWHERE ELSE, OTAY MESA

(continued from "Ahora Sí")

"**Y**ou told me to trust my woman's intuition and I'm telling you, there's drama here. We gotta cross somewhere else, *now!*" Charlie grips the wheel and takes a big breath.

"Hold on to your butts!" The tires screech mightily as he cuts through three lanes of traffic, then two more just like that. Dang, you didn't know Charlie could drive! You're barreling down the exit ramp and he takes his right hand off the steering wheel and puts on some thrash metal! The car is swerving side to side. You can't hear the screeching any more just the driving beat of the bass guitar and drums like a heartbeat on a handful of meth: crazy fast! You catch bits of the lyrics:

> *...no place to run,*
> *...only the wish to survive...*something, something
> *Come on follow us on our ride to the land of the dreams,*
> something, something
> *Tear down the wall and run for the attack!*

You look back. There are red flashing lights everywhere. You can't tell if they're getting closer. "Shit I think they're following us!"

Charlie steps on the gas. You're going seventy-five miles-per-hour on a two-lane frontage road heading somewhere. The red reflects in your mirror. Charlie is swerving back and forth facing on-coming traffic in order to cut ahead of the slow pokes. You feel your body sway like kelp in an ocean storm. You just hope your middle won't break apart. He's driving in the left lane again. You see the oncoming headlights overpowering you. Your breath is gone. You can't even scream. Everything slows down like in a dream: you feel the car edge right. You look. The lane isn't empty. There's a giant Corona Beer truck in it. The big yellow bottle gets closer and closer. It looms over you and next is the crash. You can feel it before it hits and clench your fists and feet. But then Charlie yanks you left again and you find yourselves driving between the lanes with the giant beer truck inches away and a tan SUV on your right coming toward you. You close your eyes, but you still see the headlights through your eyelids. You hear a sudden crunching sound, but you're still going forward. The SUV has passed and you're in the left lane again for two seconds while Charlie powers forward headlights growing. Then swerve, you're in the right lane as you should be, *ahead* of the beer truck, not in it, not in it.

"Oh, shit, that was some crazy driving, bro!" Fedi yells out. "Dang, you should become a professional racer or an L.A. cop or something!"

"Look back, yo. Are they still following us?

"The coast is clear, Charlie's Angel." says Pato. "You must have an angel to get us out of that mess! Where to?"

"Otay Mesa. We'll cross there. It's not too far. But I say let's pull over and chill out a bit." You do.

Back on the road, the crossing is within sight at about four in the morning. It's not as packed as the Tijuana crossing was. You notice your throat starts to close up. If it's less busy here, maybe they'll have more time to analyze the paperwork. The line is moving: stop start, stop start. Everything seems so robotic and business-like. You can't seem to stop your hands from shaking.

"This time *I'm* picking the music!" You select some Mingus tracks starting with, "Embraceable You". You need something to push your heart rate down.

"Are you kidding me, Chela? This is music for the funeral parlor!" Charlie pipes in.

"Shut up, man. It's our turn!" barks Pato. In a flash, he composes himself. The Border Patrol Agent is almost within earshot. The Agent is a muscle-bound Filipino man in his late twenties or thereabouts. He sounds very neutral when he asks for Charlie's citizenship. He is so professional as he examines Charlie's passport, you can't read him. It seems like he's about to let you go when he then asks you for your citizenship. "Mexican," you say in perfect English.

"I'd like to see your passport." You hand it to him in a flash. Then he butchers your name, your whole name, all twenty-nine letters: "Chavela Coatlicue Alvarez Santis. Sure you're not from L.A.? And your visa, Ms. Alvarez?" As you're handing it to him, the music changes to "Dance of the Infidels", a speedy sort of piece with a hyperactive alto sax lead. You notice his eyebrows jump with the shift in pace. His tone of voice changes too. "You in the back. I need to see your passports and visas too." This is it. He's going to notice that Pato doesn't have a visa or worse, he'll see that his passport expiration date is forged. Pato nudges Fedi and collects Fedi's documents then adds his own and passes the bundle over to you and you add yours to the pile and fork it over to the Agent. He examines them in the harsh floodlight. He hands back individually four of the five documents given to him. He holds Pato's passport, "Patricio Nicolás Barraza Castañeda. I need your visa too."

"Sorry, sir, I lost it. We're musicians going to play at The Pulse in Los Angeles. Here's a notarized letter from the owner." The agent takes the letter and Pato's no-good passport and walks back into the booth. This is it. You notice Charlie looking over his shoulder then putting the wagon in reverse. He goes back two yards, changes gear and *blam*! He shoots forward like a stallion itching to race. The station wagon mows through the gate barrier and takes off down the freeway. Before you know, it Border Highway Patrol vehicles are after you and you're speeding down the side of the highway like maniacs. There's a giant wall to your right so you can't just plow into the desert, not yet. You feel a pounding against your chest. It's the opening bass line from "Haitian Fight Song". Charlie must have really turned up the volume to hit you like that. The wagon is swerving on and off the highway. The shoulder is lower and you're afraid you all might tip over to scrape against the giant wall. You imagine the side of the wagon getting ripped off like in the movies. A patrol car pulls up to the left of you. They speak in a megaphone. Blurry words that have no meaning. You see the agents' faces, big eyes bulging. The music makes you think of the Tonton Macoute of Haiti surrounding the common folk and kidnapping and torturing them. But the song rears up in a flurry like a fighting cock: claws and knives implode together and ricochet off, then rear up to attack once more.

"Come on, Charlie, drive! You got this!" you scream out. You feel your head press against the seat as Charlie speeds up. You look to your right and a highway patrol car is there now.

"Holy shit! We're surrounded!" Fedi hollers. But the song keeps whopping, Fight! Fight! Fight! Charlie swerves right…as if to shove the patrol car right against the wall. The patrol car inches into the gap between you and the wall. Dang, they're good drivers! If Charlie harms CHPS by running them into the wall, you'll really be screwed. The megaphone bawls at you again. What are they saying? You see rifles pointed at you. Shit. The music keeps throbbing and you keep swerving toward them: a weaving, wandering dangerous dance you do at ninety miles per hour. You look and you see the patrol car neck and neck with your station wagon. They're going to smack right into Pato! Then Charlie shoots forward about to hit the other car and then he speeds up and swerves to the right. The patrol car had fallen behind, but is gaining on you now. Their headlights fill up your eyes. All you see is white. Then you dart directly in front of it. The screaming of their brakes is even louder than the music and you thunder out into the desert. The wall was missing a section somehow. Your station wagon bobs up and down against the terrain. Charlie attempts to brake and you start rotating and tipping to the right. But then he gains control again. Then Charlie turns off the headlights. He keeps driving that way, but much slower now. "Hey, Charlie, I see a helicopter with spotlights in the distance." Pato comments matter-of-factly. You sigh. Mingus' "I Remember April" has been playing for some time, all cool and waterlike. It helps you stay calm. "Now there's two, man. I vote we abandon the vehicle and hide. In this darkness you're lucky we haven't hit a boulder or something."

"These guys are like special-ops types. They'll find us on foot as well as in this clunker." Not too far away the helicopters crisscross each other's paths like twin spiders weaving a web. You look up into the moonless sky and see the stars. There's one you notice so much brighter than the others. It's pulsating and dancing. You decide it's cheering you on, this star in the northern sky. You look at it and you pray, asking for protection. From its lookout post, the star sees more than you will ever see. In your prayers you mention the nobility of your quest. The bass *belongs* in the hands of your family. It was made for you and not some rich kid in Palos Verdes. At the end, you promise to take more notice of the sky when you can. You can't really see it from D.F. but…the helicopters keep gaining. You feel defeated. The CD ends and there's something wrong with this stereo that won't let it repeat without you ejecting it first. Charlie drives in silence, using starlight to maneuver across the desert, avoiding gullies best he can. All it takes is one gully or big rock and the Subaru will come to a halt despite the all-wheel drive. The searchlights float closer like ghosts. The starlight is getting harder to see. Charlie keeps swerving to avoid being traced, knowing it's likely a fool's errand. The light from one of the helicopters lands three car lengths to the side of you, coming closer. You look to the right and the second helicopter is coming, too. They're about to cross paths with each other and you'll be right in the middle of their bull's-eye. "This is it, guys," Pato announces. You hold your breath. The light is almost upon you inching closer. Then out of nowhere, both helicopters swoop off toward Tijuana, somehow missing your vehicle.

"That was crazy! I can't believe they just left," says Fedi.

"Yeah, man. I thought we were goners for sure!" Charlie replies.

"We were like stealth. Black obsidian warriors!" Fedi adds.

"They must be going back to deal with whatever mess is happening over in TJ, right Chela?" Pato tries to include you.

"I don't want to talk. I don't want to say a damn thing!" At that, you put your head in your hands and breathe into them. The scent of your own breath is salty and all your own.

Turn to page 94.

THIS MORNING AT MIDNIGHT
(continued from "Ahora Sí")

"**F**ine," you say. "I guess you do have more experience crossing the border than I do."

"Yeah, and isn't that ironic? Because he's the gringo and you're the Mexican!"

You can't tell if Fedi is getting into deep political analysis here or going into stupid-comment-mode.

"Yeah, ironic," you say.

"Hey guys, we gotta spit some lyrics here," says Pato. Something like, "As we enter the valley of the flashing lights…"

"My hopes could win or lose tonight," adds in Charlie.

"Will I win this border-crossing fight? Or just slump in the corner downing shoulda, coulda, woulda and might…" Fedi can spew out some real poetry. Then he turns to you. "OK, Chela, your turn."

"I don't know, man, my mind's drawing a blank. Sorry guys." You normally love creating lyrics this way. Sometimes they end up a little goofy, but when it works, it works! Besides, the goofy songs can always be tweaked later. Pato starts to sing in English toting a thick but loveable accent:

> "*Tonight at noon, tonight at noon*
> *When we meet at the midnight hour*
> *I will bring you night flowers*
> *colored like your eyes*"

"Hey, Pato, isn't that The Jam?" Charlie asks.

"Yeah."

"That ain't no jam," Fedi insists. "Maybe if we made a Goth version." At that he starts imitating some guitar riffs.

"Yo, Fedi, there's a band *called* The Jam. They're British from the 80s. But that line is way older than that… "Tonight At Noon." I've heard that before. I think it's like a title of one of my parents' musty vinyl records…"

"Whatever, but I still say we should turn it into a Goth song. We could ramp up the tune and turn the lyrics into some kind of vampire love story. Zombies rule, but vampires are still way-in, you know?"

"As musicians," Pato starts. "We are kind of like Vampires, or nurses at the hospital." At that he chuckles. Pato's sister became a nurse and works a night shift. They often have breakfast together at two pm. "Speaking of living by night, let's cross this militarized mo-fo! Are you with me? But if you want to wait till tomorrow it's your last chance!

"Let's just do it," hollers Charlie. "Besides it would be some serious *Dukes of Hazard* type driving if we tried to get off the highway now!"

"Duke of *what*?" asks Fedi.

"Forget about it."

"OK, Valley of the Red Flashing Lights, here we go!"

When you pull up to the booth, the female Latina-looking border agent is still finishing up a call on some talking device wired to her badge. She looks up and asks each of you for your documents, following you with her eyes steady slow so you know she's checking you out, but at the same time you don't feel invaded or judged and could soon forget it even happened.

"So who is Patricio Nicolás Barraza Castañeda?" She asks, but she must know because she holds his passport and Pato has the biggest, roundest face and the thickest eyebrows of anyone there.

Pato raises his hand and gestures.

"Hello, I am Agent Salvador. My job here is almost complete. I just need your visa."

"Yes, Ma'am. Let me show you the notarized letter from Charles

Schmitt, the owner of The Pulse in Los Angeles. We're musicians on tour and he invited us to play. His club is very prestigious in our circles."

"A few years ago, Mr. Barraza, this is all you would have needed, but now due to all the terrorists trying to get into our country illegally, we have had to change our policies for the sake of everyone's safety, even yours. But I'm assuming you must have known that because all of your compatriots provided visas except you."

Charlie practically spits up his soda, but forces it down again in an awkward lurch.

"That's because mine was stolen...in Mazatlán when we did a show there for the tourists..."

"Did you report it, Mr. Barraza?"

"No...was I supposed to?"

"Absolutely! Are you really dumb enough *not* to know that? Do you realize what danger that could pose to our nation? It is probable there is someone out there with *your* visa. It could be in the hands of someone who could pass as you and with your face, that could be quite a number of people!" You look back and Pato's face looks gray in the lighting. You spot one of Fedi's clenched fists. You look back at the agent and notice her putting everyone's documents in a pouch around her waist. In her hands she holds Pato's passport.

"Well, um...Agent Salvador." Charlie starts in. "Can we still report it lost now?"

"Sure you can." And she writes down a phone number onto a card with ICE's number on it: 1-888-ILLEGAL. "But do contact the Mexican government as this poses a problem for both nations."

"At this point, would it be helpful if I call Mr. Schmitt myself?" Charlie reaches for his phone.

"No need. Your cell phone will not work here." At that, she pushes a button on her belt and soon she is joined by another officer. They talk in tense low voices together. They are looking at something, but their bodies are blocking your view. Then they pull out a portable floodlight of sorts. You squint. Part of you does not want to know what they're doing. By now, a third officer has joined them. This can't be a good sign.

"Mr. Levinson, I'll need you to follow Agent Beckwith four lanes to the left. See that building over there. You'll be parking alongside of it. Don't worry, the other lanes will be stopped for your safety and convenience." Charlie looks at you. His face is hard to read, but you sense he's squirming inside, itching to race away. Race to freedom somewhere…not here.

Turn to page 99.

CHICANO PARK

(continued from "Somewhere Else Otay Mesa")

You watch the helicopters shrink into the sky. When they're smaller than your pinky finger, you turn to Charlie and say, "Let's get the fuck out of here!" You all scramble into the wagon and Charlie takes to the paved roads once again. No one hardly talks. You're all looking out the windows, waiting for the helicopters to sweep over you again. Somehow deep in your mind it's like they're alive and can sniff out your particular heartbeat in a million. Their electronic eyes are always upon you.

You enter the city of San Diego with its wide corridors and lush gardens and scattered patches of desert alongside corporate mega-stores like Walmart. Fedi starts making annoying jokes, "Now here's the one about the Sikh, the barber and a drunk Dalmatian..." but no one is hardly listening. "Am I funny or what?"

"What, what?" barks Pato.

"OK, OK. But I got another one..."

"Enough, Fedi let *me* have a crack at it," Pato insists. "Imagine yourself in a shack, posing as a bar, out there in the middle of the countryside. Nothing much around, but cows and goats and fields. A gringo comes in and sits down. He looks out of place. The paisa next to him, wearing a faded sarape, starts up a conversation. He points at the window and says, 'You see that wall over there?' 'Yeah,' says the tourist. 'I built it con mis propias manos, every stone laid down with care! But do they call me Hernandez The Mason? No, not me!' Then he points to a shack in the distance. 'Now, see that schoolhouse?' 'Yeah,' says the gringo again. 'Well, I built it too, con mis propias manos. Split the boards using the way my great grandfather taught me. But do they call me Hernandez The Builder? No, not me!' He points for a third time. 'Look around at this bar right here. Look at the counters. Built them, con mis propias manos. But do they call me Hernandez The Woodworker? No, not me!' He looks around, his eyes open wide, and places his face right in front of the Gringo and says, '...but you fuck one goat...'" You and Charlie start cracking up. Even Fedi breaks into a smile despite having lost the battle of the word.

"I guess that's true," says Charlie. "You always remember someone for their fuckup, not for all the good things they've done."

"Yeah, what's up with that?" chimes in Fedi.

"Some things shouldn't be forgiven," says Pato in a very final voice. A moment of silence follows.

"Hey, yo, we're almost at my buddy's turf." Charlie parks the Subaru next to a large park dissected by mad freeway overpasses. At least the people decorated them with fucking amazing murals. Puro Chicanismo. You look up to see Frida, Zapata and Cesar Chávez staring at you.

You all get out. "You can all chill." Charlie says. "I'm gonna call my buddy Killer."

"Killer?" you ask.

"Oh, that's just a nickname. He was into some things back in the day. An O.G. of sorts, but he's got a fucking college degree and..."

"If he's college educated, then why not drop the name?" says Pato. "Killer? Sounds like he still has one foot into that life. We're supposed to *trust* him?"

"No worries. I've known him for years. We've gotta ditch this car for a spell. I've had enough helicopters following me to last a lifetime, a que no?"

You and Fedi start to wander around together. Pato sticks by

Charlie. You guess he doesn't trust this Killer character and doesn't trust Charlie's judgment either.

The park is an explosion of colors; so many murals crammed into such a small space thriving on the most hideous structures like freeway pillars. The images of indigenous heroes and barrio warriors demanding their rights are welcoming. Fedi is in heaven. "Look, Chela, check out that warrior! Damn, she's got muscles. Look at that zoot suiter, yeah, I'm gonna get me a chain like that! And there you are, Coatlicue…looking bad-assed."

You find the city of murals at the park to be affirming, but not welcoming. This park has a sort of edgy feel to it on a weekday in the middle of the day. There's no grammas and babies strolling. No naïve twerpy kid doing their thing. It's pretty ghost towny in the present moment. Pato finds you. "Well guys, *Killer* is on his way."

"I wanna check out *that* dude!" says Fedi. "Just sniff him out. I don't have to even talk to him!"

"Well, Charlie trusts him and Charlie has good sense…pretty good anyway," you add. Over toward the green side of the park there's a hollow pyramid looking structure instead of the typical trellised gringo bandstand. You notice a man lurking behind it. He's tall and big-boned. He's wearing a grimy LA Angels cap and pushing a shopping cart. He cuts around the backside of the pyramid. You start talking to Pato and Fedi some more about this Killer character and who he might end up being and forget about Shopping-Cart-Man. You go on talking until you hear an abrupt crinkly sound. You turn your head to see Shopping-Cart-Man rock his foot over a plastic pop bottle, crushing it instantly and giving off that eerie crinkly sound. In a flash he takes a broom handle with a nail sticking out of one end and–without bending down–pierces the bottle and tosses it in the cart to join his collection of flattened bottles, cans and stuffed animals coated in soot. Then down goes the next bottle and so on. You notice his left hand is a prosthetic, a claw. It doesn't hinder his efficiency.

"Boy, I'm glad he has the *other* hand to pick his nose with and… well anyways."

"Shut up Fedi. I don't want to think about *that*! Where are we anyway, Pato?"

"Chicano Park." You just look at him. "Barrio Logan." You look at him twice. "San Diego, Chela. Look at the murals; there's signs about territory everywhere: Barrio Logan this. Aztlán that, La Tierra Mia…without the accent of course. Come on, *some* Chicanos must know their basic accent rules, right?"

Shopping-Cart-Man almost silently passes by you all. It's like he's in some kind of parallel universe. Like he's a Tarahumara down from the mountains, not engaged in the same social conventions most Mexicans embody. The Tarahumaras you met always seemed to be more buoyant than everyone else. The man is about to float on by when you catch him staring at Pato. By now, Pato's back is turned and Fedi is talking on and on about what songs he wants to play at The Pulse. As the man stares at Pato, and suddenly he seems so solid, full of earthly longing. You wonder if his face reflects your own. You're trying to hide your desperation to get to Palos Verdes, to hold the Perfumed Lady in your arms. You look at the mini beads of sweat gathering on his shiny copper-colored brow. You touch your own face. It's damp, too. This guy is some kind of trickster. You half expect him to pull out a bottle of snake oil and bust out with a sales pitch. You look down at your feet for a while. It's safe there. When you look back up, he's gone, totally gone.

"What's up?" Pato asks. "Who are you staring at?"

"Just some random guy. He just reminded me of something."

"Hey, Chela, we gotta be in L.A. by tomorrow. Our gig is tomorrow, dude. Fedi wants to play that death metal cover of 'Fire Water Burn' and also our cover of Maná's 'Amor Clandestino.'"

"Sure, whatever."

"I thought you hated those songs, Chela!"

"I don't care anymore. It's all good."

"For realz?"

"Yeah, I mean it. You choose. I'll play whatever you want except for the 'Star Spangled Banner.'"

"What do you mean? Hendrix rocked that back in the old days!"

"True. You got me there! I guess you know your guitar hero history."

"Thanks, Chela, but…you're different. What happened to the player-hating opinionated Chela I finally learned to like?" asks Fedi.

"Hey, I'm on vacay!" Everyone snickers. In the distance you see Charlie with what looks like a vato from the movies. He isn't ethereal like the Cart-Man. He's solid and this is his turf and whatever happens next, you all will be playing by his rules. That's for sure.

Turn to page 105.

> "I'm going to keep on finding out
> the kind of man I am through my music.
> That's the one place I can be free."
>
> *Charles Mingus*

ICE SO COLD

(continued from "This Morning at Midnight")

There seems to be no way out. The government cars around you appear like a shifting wall of metal, a prison of sorts. There is a small opening to your left. You go to it. Then another opening further to your left. You drive into that space. Then another and another and before you know it, the station wagon arrives at exactly the spot the agent specified.

They order you all out of the vehicle. Bring your wallets and personal bags. Leave your other things behind for now. Armed officers take you to a room. It's stark with white pleather benches and pale green walls, which could be on account of the hideous fluorescent lights dangling above you. It's like there's some hyper-clean seeming residue coating all you touch or see. Maybe the air conditioning is pushing microdust around. It's cranked on all the way. You all sit there in silence until an agent comes to confirm everyone's name, pokes at his iPad and then leaves. After a long while, Charlie speaks:

"Sorry, guys, I was so sure this would work out. It used to be a cinch to cross. I mean, no one here looks like the typical migrant. We're a band on tour for fuck's sake."

An armed agent comes and calls out Pato's name. He takes him away.

"What's up with *that?*" asks Fedi.

"Shhh. They're probably listening to us in here." Then a heavily armed female agent comes and takes Charlie away. You look over at Fedi. It's just the two of you. There are so many things you've wanted to say to him, alone without an audience. You've wanted to chew him out for being an arrogant asshole, yet you want to embrace him for taking a stand with those crazy nuns; you want to cry for all the heckling he's dished out over the years and still you want to thank him for at least half of it cuz him calling out your shit has made you a better person. But fuck, they're listening. You know they are. So you don't say shit. Instead, you nudge over closer and lay your head in his lap and close your eyes. He strokes your hair here and there, but not in a creepy way. The cold air keeps you from really sleeping. Oh, well.

Then they bring Charlie back. You see the trails of dried tears down his face. His words come out in a gasping tumble, "Pato is in some big fucking trouble. They say he forged his passport. They want to pin me for willingly transporting illegals across the border."

"But you *didn't know*. You thought everything was cool…like we all did." You swallow loudly.

"I tried to tell them that, but then they said according to the Immigration and Nationality Act, it doesn't matter if I knew. I was being *reckless* by not checking everyone's passport. But I said, 'I'm American, how do I know what Mexican passports are supposed to look like?' And that's the truth. I didn't know. I mean Pato is always the together one. He's like the grandfather of the group. I would never imagine that he would try to cross the border with a forged passport…"

"Well, you don't know if that's even true, Charlie. I mean, they could be trying to pin that on him cuz they don't like the way he looks!"

"OK, OK. You got me there. I shouldn't assume what they're saying is right…"

"Yeah, man," starts Fedi, "What you should be talking about is how to get Pato out of this mess!"

Fedi is right. Pato could be in some serious trouble.

"But if it were true," Charlie can't stop himself, "then he was really taking a serious risk having a falsified passport just to play some gigs."

"Sometimes, Charlie, you gotta go for the gold no matter what!"

Fedi's philosophy is not exactly comforting considering Pato probably didn't care that much about going for the gold by playing at The Pulse, but instead was going for the gold heart. He did it for you to get the Perfumed Lady back. You feel your chest cave in. You consider telling them the whole crazy story...all of it. Nah.

This time they come for you. They pummel you with questions: *Who are you? What kind of trip were you planning in the US? Had you been before? Where exactly were you planning on playing? Did you know you were only allowed to go a certain number of miles north of the border or violate your visa?* You hadn't even crossed the border and already you were violating a visa. Later come the heavier questions: *Did you know that Pato forged his passport? What kind of person was Pato? Did you know where Pato's father was living?* Then he hits you with the nice tone: *Think back to your conversations with Pato over the years where he may have mentioned his father...*What? you ask yourself. What father? Wasn't he dead? After a while you get it: They think that Pato is the mastermind and had planned a trip where he would cross the border under the guise of going on tour so that he could reunite with his deadbeat dad who was living in Barrio Logan, wherever that is. You tell him you thought Pato had no idea where his dad was and that to your knowledge he lightweight hated the man. They insist Pato had known he was in San Diego and that Pato knew about his father's anarchistic leanings. They had arrested him multiple times, but he always escaped unscathed until the last time.... They pause to look at you when they say this last bit. They go on about how he paid a price, but managed to worm his way out of the handcuffs. The questions thunder on and you find yourself drifting off, not listening well, no, not hardly listening at all. They keep insisting that Pato used you. He was not the loyal friend he seemed to be. If only you would give them more information about Pato then you could go free. They try to break you, but it doesn't work. Moments surge when you're itching to tell them the real truth: that *you're* the foolish mastermind, the one that got *him* to follow *you*. They won't believe you anyhow...you'd just be wasting your breath.

Besides, you had the correct paperwork, not he. They don't really have anything on you. Why should you *both* wind up in trouble?

"Miss Chavela Coatlicue Alvarez Santis! Are you listening to what I'm saying?"

"Huh? Um, yeah. I'm just really tired." Your body aches all over with want of sleep, but you still can't imagine relaxing in such cold air after being yelled at half the night. Your wrists hurt from those damned zip-tie cuffs.

"Well, you won't be resting for a while."

"What do you mean? You're letting me go, right?"

"Not immediately. Your case is more complicated than we first expected."

"Complicated? But I have all my proper documents!"

"That you may have, but you were still aiding and abetting an illegal immigrant who was breaking both Mexican and American law by having a forged passport. In addition, he had no visa, something he must have known he would have needed because you two brought yours, didn't you?"

"Aiding and abetting a what? But he didn't actually immigrate did he? He's not an immigrant. He never stepped foot on American turf, did he?"

"He has now. This is *American* land you're standing on, too. You've entered the Fifty States."

"But you brought us here!" It makes no sense, but the argument is pointless. The immigration agent has the power and you don't have shit. You turn to him with fire in your eyes. "Well some people have great-great-grandparents who could have stood on this very spot when it was *Mexican*!" You feel the sudden chill roll down your back. You can't believe what you just said.

"It doesn't serve you to romanticize the past. This is American soil now. The laws you must abide by are the *current* ones, not laws from one hundred sixty years ago…"

"Well my laws run deeper than that!"

"Miss Alvarez, I think the best thing you could do now is to refrain from talking out of turn. Like I said, you're in serious trouble and yet still you won't tell us anything about your best friend Pato's father."

"I don't know anything! He's dead."

"How can that be? You're his friend, his *best* friend."

"No I'm not! I'm just using him, OK? I'm using him so I can get to L.A. He thought I was his friend, but I'm not…I'm just a spoiled brat, OK and I dragged him here all because I wanted to buy a bass in Los Angeles." You're panting.

"I hate to burst your bubble, but that does not exactly sound realistic. Maybe you should have gone to acting school instead of music school. Don't you realize what's at stake here? Would you really risk your future to purchase an instrument in a foreign country? Why not ship it? Surely such a thing could be done safely without all the bother of dragging three other people across México and into all of this mess. Sorry, I just don't buy that."

You feel your eyes start to swell as tears rush through. Shipping? The ad said no shipping. No exceptions…. You were afraid he would give it to an American to save himself the bother. Shipping, why didn't anyone insist the jerk-off ship it? Not your uncle, not Pato, not you. As much as your friends made fun of your relative privilege, it didn't occur to you to bargain with the seller. You should have told your mother what you were doing. She would have thought of a way to help you negotiate shipping with the American seller. She would have. The shortcut was waiting for you all along.

You feel a pressure building in your eyes, till the tears break through your pores. They flow down your red cheeks. Your face swells. Your neck clenches tight. The agent leaves you to your sorrow in that ice-cold place on *American* soil. You hold the handle of the locked door to the room and start banging your head against it. The aches refresh your senses, urging you to tip your head forward again and again. You bang until they come for you and take you away.

You end up in an immigrant detention center on the outskirts of Tijuana. The yard is co-ed and you hear whimpering from dark corners. You know what's happening there and that it's just a matter of time before you, too, will be raped by several men at once. It's more like a camp than a jail. You find Fedi. He vows to protect you.

You pretend you're a couple with him. He looks tough and in actuality he is quite tough, he's just been hiding it since the day he chose God and guitar. But now he's got watch over you. There are people who have been there over nine months and never been formally accused, never seen a judge…not yet. You look and look, but Pato is not there. "He's probably in a real jail," Fedi says and you know he's likely right. You wonder what happened to Charlie. You imagine they freed him and he's trying to get visitation with you, a lawyer…something. Fedi thinks he's locked up, too. "I feel it, Chela. It's like we're twins. He's locked up just like we are, but he'll get his phone call and all that."

"Do you think we'll ever see him?"

"Sure we will. He's gonna come for us. I'm sure of it, Chela. He won't abandon us. It's Pato I'm worried about…"

"I know, me, too."

"Hey Chela, you know it could be worse."

"Yeah? What would be worse?"

"Being locked up and never seeing the sky. Look, I can see a big fat star over there. Look, it's flickering. It's a drunken star, Chela. Look, don't you see it? It's gone crazy…it's like it's trying to give us a message. Chela, I'm telling you God sent us an angel. Look, Chela. Look up goddamnit, the star, the star!"

This is a dead end.

Turn back to an earlier page and choose another path.

KILLER

(continued from "Chicano Park")

You try not to look like you're sizing up this Killer character. You notice his shoulders are stiff and rolled back. His body movements are minimal. His clothing is even stiffer than his body. He's wearing a brown Pendleton and stunna' shades. His shoes look brand spanking new, so new they're unreal. His eyes show no emotion. You wonder how much blood he has had to walk through in his life, blood spilt of his own doing. You turn to look at Fedi. He's posturing, craning his neck. Great, all you all need is a fight now.

Charlie tries to cut through the tension, "Hey, yo, this is my buddy..."

"Joaquín. You can call me Joaquín." His words are friendly, but then he crosses his arms in a cold street-thug kind of way.

"Thanks for offering to help us," Pato says. What a diplomat!

"Sure, the pleasure is all mine. Me 'n Charlie go way back." His arms are still crossed. He wears a long sleeved shirt under his tee you imagine to cover up all the breasts and bandoliers, saints and skulls inked on his skin.

"So where's the car?" Fedi sounds a little jumpy. Normally he plays it cooler than this. You look up at Killer's glassy hazel eyes. His skin is a pasty café con lots of leche. It looks like he hasn't been in the sun much or more like he has armor, armor that won't tan or burn or react in any way to ultraviolet rays.

"It's around the corner. No worries. The plates are fake. There's no VIN. There's no history. It's like this car appeared out of nowhere."

"But of course it didn't." Pato says calmly.

"Well, only God and magicians can make something appear out of nowhere, a que sí?" You want to ask him which he thinks he is. He sounds more like a snake-oil salesman to you. But you stay quiet.

"Hey, look guys!" Charlie pulls a flip phone out of his pocket. "Communication! Part of the perks of the deal!"

"Deal?" Pato's eyebrows are stuck in a half-raised position. His body is stone still.

"So let me tell you how it's going to work," Charlie says, smiling and detracting from the rising tension. "We gotta unload our car stashed in a garage up the way and load up the new car with our gear. We go on tour, do our thing and next week, while we're on our way back, we'll stop off at the garage to return our car and so I can get my old one back...."

"The same garage?" interrupts Fedi.

"No, a different one. That's way better in case we're being traced somehow. Killer's dudes...I mean Joaquín's associates may trick it out so it will be unrecognizable to the border pigs for our reentry into México. By then, I'm hoping that the heat will be off. The beauty of it is Kil...Joaquín is not even going to charge us. He's gonna actually give us some gas money..."

You notice Killer uncrossing his arms.

"Yo, I really believe in what you all are doing," Killer interjects. "Musically I mean. I like your style...the mixing of thrash beats and oldies. Glad you got that hip-hop in there. I'm a big fan of the oldies and jazz, too, but of course I gotta stay contemporary. You know, keep up with what's hot."

"And besides gas money," Charlie goes on like he's reading some script. "He's going to send a buddy with us to be our roadie and manage our merch."

"What?" asks Pato.

"Yeah, who's this roadie guy?" Fedi adds.

"One of my associates. His name is Armando. He may be short, but he can lug quite a load. Like I said, Charlie and I go way back. Anything to help a friend."

"Hey, I've met Armando, he's pretty cool. Pato, I thought you'd be psyched to save your back this time." Charlie is smiling large. "The only catch is that Armando has to make a pit stop in Boyle Heights. That's in L.A."

Pato raises an eyebrow. "Well, I guess we don't have much choice do we? I mean, we can't be seen in the Subaru, not after the Migra has been chasing us by helicopter 'n shit. Did Charlie tell you what it took for us to get here?"

"A little," Killer answers. "Sounds like you been through some crazy shit, homes, we're talking Homie's Odyssey…"

"You went to college with Charlie, right? What did you major in?" you ask.

"Poli Sci with a minor in Justice Studies. I'd love to talk more, but we gotta get moving. Time is of the essence."

"Speaking of getting moving, I've got my own pit stop to make and now. It's a woman thing." You look down at the sidewalk. You didn't really mean to share so much. "I need to get to a pharmacy." You look at Charlie. "You know your way around here. Can you go with me?"

"I think that should be okay. You guys can handle switching over the gear, right. Plus, Armando can help you."

"Sure, boss," snaps Fedi. Charlie gives him a look. You scratch the bottom of your palms with your two middle fingers. It's a weird habit typical of babies and old men. You and Charlie head out in search of feminine hygiene products while Pato and Fedi go over to the garage with Killer. You don't look back. You don't wanna see Pato's face. Normally, *he* would accompany you on such an errand. You're practical. You don't want to end up walking in circles in this neighborhood.

"Hey, Chela, you know you don't actually have to go to a *pharmacy* in the US to get what you're getting. A corner store would do the trick."

"Whatever. I want to walk at least a kilometer. I need a break from the other guys. Besides, I wanna shoot the shit a little."

Turn to page 112.

TÍA'S HOSPITALITY

(continued from "Tía Juana")

"OK. Let's go check out Pato's tía…. Eh?"

"Tía María!" pipes in Fedi.

"Yeah, funny. Don't be saying that around my tía. She'll smack you upside the head and make you repent to a priest on top of it. You can call her Doña Dominga."

Doña Dominga's house is simple and compact, compared to many of the others. Made of cinderblocks but tiled over with glossy Italian tile in colors that don a dash more vibrant than neutrals. Really, you could have looked this house over and not realized it. Even the pre-fabricated Virgen de Guadalupe tiles, eight in all, next to the built-in niche is very unoriginal, though sweet in its way. A spent candle and dried flowers prove the niche is not just for appearances.

Doña walks out the door to greet you before Charlie is finished parking. She is tall and big-boned like Pato. She kind of looks like a retired wrestler; I mean, this woman is built. She has big eyes and a tight mouth like Christian Martyrs in religious paintings. Her greeting to you is the briefest possible to still be considered polite within Mexican customs and bordering on rude considering there is a gringo in your midst. When you get to the dining room table, hot chocolate is already served in mugs. It's still piping. You try to figure out how she could have poured those cups and stepped outside all while you were pulling up. It doesn't follow.

"Patricio, I need to talk to you." Pato's body looks like a hunk of clay without fine tools to shape it. "You know who it's about…"

Pato snaps into movement. "Sure, Tía. I'll be right back, guys." They go off into the next room.

Fedi hisses, "What's up with that?"

"Family matters, I guess." But you don't buy your own explanation. You're just gulping down the last bit of hot chocolate when Pato emerges. His eyes look puffy, but it's hard to say. Suddenly, Doña Dominga is friendly, almost fakely so. She shows you around the place, offers you pan dulce, then she tells stories about when Pato was little and how sensitive he used to be, especially when it came to animals. He was always bringing stray animals home and nursing them back to health, sometimes secretly, keeping them in a closet. "You never knew where he'd have one stashed. I remember I kept hearing croaking somewhere in the house back when I lived in the country. Turns out he had a frog held prisoner in a little box under the floor boards."

Pato turns to us. "It was hurt."

"Of course it was. You always wanted to fix things, didn't you?" You wonder if this is double-speak. If you all are the broken thing or the strays.

Doña Dominga's house is small, but she manages to find bedding for everyone. Before you know it, the sun is rising and you all start milling about, readying to leave. She serves Mexican coffee, weak with cinnamon, fried eggs and tortillas and the remaining pan dulce. You watch as Pato almost clings to her as he embraces her. You watch, as if you were holding to her, too. She sheds a tear now. *What is going on?* You've got to find out.

You repack the car. You had taken everything out just a few hours before in case of robbery. Somehow the items do not fit right and your legs are crammed in front along with a box of your band's CDs and Fedi's backpack. As you head toward the rising sun, you think of what is rising for you…a show at an awesome club, a chance to hold the Perfumed Lady in your arms, to take in her scent, to feel Abuelita Sálome again almost in the flesh…and you hope, you sure hope that what is rising for you is not, in actuality, trouble at the border.

Turn to page 117.

SHOOT THE SHIT

(continued from "Killer")

"**S**o what's up? What do you want to talk about?"

"You."

"OK." He looks a little puzzled. "Well shoot."

"I don't know how to say this. I'm normally so crazy blunt, but I don't want to hurt your feelings so…"

"Hurt my feelings?"

"Look, Charlie. I'm seeing all these different sides to you. I knew from the get-go that you weren't born talking the way you talk, but over the years, I got used to you talking like that and I figured, *that's just Charlie.*"

"What do you mean, that's just street talk, keeping it real…"

"But it's not real. You're not real. You're not Mexican, man, you're white…"

"I'm Jewish…"

"OK, so you're an American from New York and here you've been talking like you're a naco from Mexico City."

"That's the crew I run with. We're family down there. So what if my blood family talks different than how you think I should be talking. And besides, Chela, you talk like that, too, and you're not a naca. You're educated."

You wait to cross a busy street before speaking. You have no idea where you are or even if you're in a different neighborhood by now.

"But I am Mexican from *The City* not the suburbs…but that's not even my point, Charlie, let me finish. Like I was trying to say…" You give him a look. "I accepted *that Charlie,* the one that tried to sound naco, and after a while it was like you were one of us, a brother…but always a follower. To be honest, I didn't respect you the way I respect Pato cuz he stands up for what he believes in. Then when you stood up to Fedi at the chop shop…I mean, that must have been the first time you ever stood up to him! Then you were like breaking down all this history and shit and I was thinking, *who is this guy?* He's so much more than what I knew. Then here we are on your turf, but don't you tell me this is where *you're from* either! I don't know what you're trying to prove acting all ghetto hanging with these banger losers."

"It's not an act. I ran with this guy in college."

"In college? I can't imagine him at UC San Diego with you hanging out in the student lounge or whatever!"

"We took half a class together…"

"*Half* a class?"

"That's when I dropped out."

"Dropped out?"

"It's a long story. I just have one more credit to go!"

"Oh, my God, Charlie! That's just what I'm talking about!" You're yelling by now! "You are meant for more than this shit! Not only do you have opportunities others would die for, you have greatness in you! I saw it in you, you fucking jerk! You just hide it! You squash it. You stomp it down!" You duck your head waiting for him to lash his tongue at you, but he doesn't. Instead he stops you from walking forward. You're both standing on the sidewalk in front of a closed storefront. He holds your shoulders and looks at you. You stare into his different colored eyes. He kind of looks like a freak in a beautiful sort of way. His lips, still swollen from the fight, appear like an angel child's. You find yourself leaning in closer and closer to him.

"Come this way. I wanna take you some place." At that, he leads you by the shoulder and then by the hand. Along the straight, generic looking streets, he sweeps you between two buildings. There is an iron gate in the middle of the breezeway. In a flash he tinkers it open. He takes you through another door and you're in a laundry room to the adjacent apartment building. He locks the door from the inside and draws the blinds over the lonely window. He draws your hand and kisses it making his way up your arm. You're thinking, *Oh, yeah, what a gentleman!* But before you know it, your neck feels all prickly. You turn to him and reach out with both of your hands and grab the shaggy edges of his overgrown muttonchops and brush your lips against his. He doesn't flinch. Must not hurt too bad. He rubs his lips playfully against yours and then gives you prissy kisses, sucking your lip in the tiniest of ways, pulling, then letting go and pulling again. You feel a tugging in your chest drawing you closer. You crane your head up and he floods your neck with little butterfly bites that pinch you and wake up your senses. He finds his way under your shirt. You like how his hands wrap around you, leave you no place to hide.

"Damn, Chela, you smell good!"

"Shut up." You pull away.

"No seriously. I like a woman with a full-bodied smell."

"That's not all I got that's full-bodied."

"Yeah, and I like that, too. Come here." At that he yanks you toward him. You sink into him and him into you. It's like you're sleep-walking and slow dancing together. His skin is warm. You savor his salty neck as you kiss it tenderly. It's softer than you expected, like girl skin, a softness you know. "Here." He grabs a large oval woven pink bathroom mat and throws it on the ground. He dips you back and places you there before sliding himself on top of you. It must be clean at least. It smells like extra strength generic Tide plus ten million sheets of rose scented fabric softener. You find yourself going along with the oddness of this whole scene. Why not? Your shirt is off by now and he's rubbing and sucking on your breasts, but not the way most guys do like they're sucking their mothers'. No, he's aiming to please. He's working your nipples in circles and repetitions of lick, suck, tug and bite. Then he's flattening them down with his tongue and pressing in deep. Meanwhile his hands surround you again, kneading you into shapes. Then he drags his lips and tongue slow and hard, down down down until his tongue melts into you.

You see blackness, rich and close like the beginnings of life. Then he rocks you, slow like a cradle at first. You could sway forever in his vaivén. His motions keep you guessing how and when he'll make it to each touchy spot of your anatomy. You can't believe how he can work you and how you're just going with it floating down this river, a slow-paced samba shifting the flow of your blood. The river flows and grows and samba speeds up making a swelling of water till there's a full-on flood busting through the banks sending explosions of rivulets upon the land, giving drink to revolutionary conspirators out in the forest. You lay there as the aftershocks flow through you.

"Damn, Carlitos...I didn't know..."

"It's the clarinet. My folks made me take clarinet. They hoped I'd be the next Benny Goodman. Hey, you gotta admit working on my embouchure all those years did wonders for my oral muscles."

You chuckle. "Are you gonna thank your parents? You should. You gringos need to show some respect for your elders!"

Charlie smiles. "Yeah, like you. You barely talk to your mom these days. Your mom is hella dope the way she protected your uncle from those thugs. She had them running!"

He saunters over to the plastic washbasin and washes his face and hands. His collar ends up stained pink. "Wait, why did I bother washing. We didn't *finish*, did we?"

"We can finish later...maybe somewhere a little more classy since I am a *fresa* after all."

"You don't like the laundry? How about a roof top somewhere?"

"Alright."

At that, his phone starts screeching with some hideous personalized ring-tone. "Holy Shit! We gotta get back to the boys. Armando should be there by now..."

"Yeah, you might need to mediate something. I just hope he's not some shady thugster."

"Yeah, me too. But think of a better way to switch out our vehicle *and* get it back later."

"Look, I don't know what to say. Do desperate times lead to

fucked up choices? Or do fucked up choices lead to fucked up choices? There's more I gotta tell you about this tour. I had ulterior motives…"

"Don't trip, Chela! We all got motives. We're in it now. We're in it deep."

———————⌇———————

Turn to page 120.

CROSSING AT RUSH HOUR

(continued from "Tía's Hospitality")

"It would be kinda cool to be a Muslim."

"What did you say, Fedi?" you ask.

"I mean, look at this sunrise, Chela. If I was a Muslim, I'd be praying on my carpet every morning and I'd always be appreciating..."

"Appreciating what?"

"To be alive. To honor the presence of God. To remember there's more out there than all the crap that's floating around in my mind! Don't chu get it?"

"No, I don't get it. I thought you were this devout Catholic."

"That's the beauty of it, Chela...there's overlap. Both honor Abraham and Moses. OK, so the Muslims see Jesus as a prophet not a savior, but I can hang with that. Besides, if I'm a Sufi then I could be Catholic *and* practice Sufism. It's more about how you are in the world and..."

"What's stopping you then, shit!" says Pato. "Get on your knees and pray, son!" Everybody snickers.

Your mind drifts into childhood recollections of your grand-mother Sálome.

You can see her getting up in the wee hours of the morning to greet the sun. The sound of her rattle would wake you. Then you'd creep over to watch her for about five minutes before going back to bed and snuggling up with your rag doll.

You never asked what it meant to her. As a kid, you didn't need

117

to. You could understand without words and now you don't get shit. It's like all the threads of connectivity between people got slashed as soon as you went into puberty. The only people you connect to are your instruments and your tío Gonzalo...OK and Pato, too. You think about the bass and how you want to hold her. You wonder if your grandmother ever touched her. You wonder what energy got transferred between those two ladies Rivera laid his hands on at that time. You notice you're not moving. "Hey Charlie, where are we?"

"About four kilometers from the border."

"Four kilometers? We're not moving."

"That's right. This is rush hour." Everyone groans.

"You all are such a sad bunch...you're pissing in each other's pozole!" Pato attempts to break the depressive mood.

You trudge along for maybe an hour; at last, the gates are in sight. You're about to meet the angels of judgment or something.

"OK everyone, remember your lines." Pato had made everyone rehearse what they were going to say at the border. It's amazing how much he knows. The gates grow larger until the overhang is already above you. You know they are probably weighing your vehicle and X-ray scanning it right now. How creepy. The agent is a young mestizo male, probably straight, but you can tell he had his eyebrows cleaned up.

"Citizenship?"

"American." Charlie says in his most middleclass gringo accent.

"U.S." you muster. You don't sound too bad.

"OK, but what about the guys in the back?" There is a long pause. "I'm going to have to ask you to declare your citizenship and provide the appropriate documents."

"They're from Mexico City. Our band is on tour," Charlie adds, trying to sound smooth.

Fedi hands up his documents prematurely since there was a chance he would not have really wanted them. The agent snaps them up with greedy precision. "Federico Martinez?"

"Yes," he replies.

The agent puts his walkie-talkie to his lips. "Donnie, come down here pronto." Another agent appears, a Mr. Donald Jameson. "Hey check it out Donnie, this is Federico Martínez..."

"Oh," he says in a cool voice. "The one that's been flagged."

The agent cracks a grin. "Yeah. That one. This is the guy from Bang Data!"

"Yeah, it's him all right."

"Well actually, I was only..." Fedi starts up. Pato crushes his foot with his giant foot to shut him up.

"What do you say Donnie, we can't let these guys through the border." The first agent winks and pauses for a while. "Not without Mr. Martinez's autograph!" They both start chuckling.

At that cue, you start rummaging through the bag at your feet. When you dig two CDs out, you notice the agents have their hands on their weapons. You stutter, "He can sign these for you." Their tense faces relax into smiles once more. Fedi signs the CDs pronto and you're off up The I-5. You're in California.

"That was easy!" remarks Charlie. "Let's go get some carne asada fries, I know a twenty four-hour place."

"I need a beer," says Pato. "No, tequila. Let's go to a bar man." No one argues. You would rather see Pato eat carne asada fries over beer for the sake of his blood sugar, but whatever works.

Turn to page 129.

MEETING ARMANDO
(continued from "Shoot The Shit")

You barely notice the scenery about you as you whiz through the neighborhood…going so fast you could never find that place again: the hidden laundromat. It gets swallowed up by the stucco uniformity of that hood.

"Hey Charlie, did you *plan* that?"

"What? What we did? No. I didn't even see it coming."

"You practically lured me into that back-alley laundromat."

"Nah, the moment arose that's all. Besides, I thought you weren't into dudes."

"Really? Oh. What made you think that?"

"I hate to tell you; everybody knows about your expulsion from the Academy. Don't take it personally. I mean that's primo gossip."

"Well, why can't a girl be with both men and women. What's wrong with that?

"Nothing. There's nothing wrong with it."

"Shit, I'm only twenty-one; don't I get time to figure this stuff out?"

"Yeah, Chela, of course you do."

"Well then, if you thought I wasn't into dudes then why did you take me to the plush laundry palace over there?"

"I don't know. The stuff you said changed how I think about you.

It was like you really *saw* me. I haven't felt that before, not even from my fucking parents, OK?"

You notice a harsh high tone surface in his voice.

"Even though I was regañándote?"

"Yeah, even with that."

You don't say any more.

You buy the tampons at a liquor store, of all places. They won't let you use the bathroom for that, but you give an embarrassed smile at the Mexican bakery and they lead you to the employee bathroom, no questions asked. When you finally arrive at the garage, everyone is standing outside leaning on the slide-door van. If these guys are supposed to be experts in car swapping, then why stand outside where everyone can see the goings down? You shrug. You turn your eyes toward the new guy. He must be Armando. He's standing apart from the group, his mouth in a straight line like it was drawn on. He's making up for every centimeter he lacks in height by standing super stiffly, sorta military-like. You notice a large blue Southpole backpack with wanna-be graffiti letters on it. It's stuffed full. Full of what? You hope he's a clotheshorse, but somehow his stark appearance gives him the minimalist kind of vibe. Besides, he's not planning on making a pit stop in Boyle Heights just to do laundry.

"Hey slow pokes, check out our new ride," says Fedi. Behind him is a nondescript white Econoline van with plain pleather seats. They have no seams, no folds, no piping. It's all very institutional looking.

Killer looks over at you. "That's our special DNA reduction covering. It's easier to clean and harder for your epithelials to get stuck in little nidos."

You nod your head with pursed lips.

You all pile in and hit the road. Luckily you're in the front. You peek at Armando through the rear-view mirror here and there. He stays looking out the window, commando-hard body language. After a few miles or so, you're already on the I-5. You had heard about the crazy freeway connections in SoCal from Charlie, so you expected to take like ten different freeways.

"Hey, Fedi, Check it out. See that big old house over there, that's where those Christiano cultistas killed themselves." You're surprised Pato recognizes the geography.

"Yeah, what of it? Don't generalize, man! Not all Christians are about to drink some poisoned Tampico Cooler or whatever."

Pato is sitting next to Armando. Fedi presses his head against the window and does not exchange glances with him at all. Pato strikes up a conversation. "So what do you like better, San Diego or L.A.?

It takes a while for Armando to answer. "L.A., I guess."

"You from there?"

"No."

A long stiff pause follows. Pato clears his throat as if to prepare for bombarding the stoic little fellow with questions. "Apatzingán Michoacán."

"Oh, we went there for our fifth grade fieldtrip, birth of the constitution and all. Changed a lot these days since then from what I hear."

"Yeah, that's true."

"Is it true that Fernando Tazón is running things down there?"

"Dunno. Haven't been in a while."

"But surely you're in touch with someone down there...skyping or email or a phone call now and then..."

"No, I'm not in touch." Pato leaves him alone after that.

Twenty minutes later, Armando opens his mouth. "Hey, Charlie, get off at Grande Vista. It'll be up in like two minutes."

Before you know it, you're turning down avenues and boulevards. The streets are wide. Sections are urban with regal Italian-style buildings. Other sections sport rows of aging little stucco bungalows like some American dream sitting in the sun too long. The famous L.A. skyline is just over to your left, not that you're super impressed by it. A bunch of tall buildings, so what?

"Pull over. Pull over by those apartments over there. Right in front."

You feel your stomach lurch. The apartments are four stories high, with peeling teal paint and gray trim. They take up one half of the block. A rusted wrought-iron fence almost three meters tall separates the apartments from the street. You wonder why there are so many available parking spaces right in front of this mega apartment complex. Doesn't everybody in L.A. have a car or two? Armando puts his bag on one shoulder and wobbles out of the car. The bag isn't all that big, but he's so short, it looks bigger. He punches a code into the call box and is buzzed in. He walks to the right. You jump out the car and over to the edge of the fence. You peer in. There's a large cement courtyard in the middle decorated by a burned up sofa. You notice beer bottles and spray-painted gang tags all over the place. Fuck. Armando is gone and anyone could see you. But you can't see shit. It's so still. Where are all the people? You hear your breathing get shallow and faster. It's like a ghost town, but *someone* buzzed him in. There must be eighty apartments, but it's so fucking empty, so fucking quiet. Something's wrong. You notice something moving up top the roof. There's someone up there. A sniper? You have a choice, to take off running to your left, the opposite direction Armando went, or slowly back up to the van and alert the others.

———————〜———————

If you choose to run away, turn to page 124.

If you choose to back up and warn the others, turn to page 126.

RUN

(continued from "Meeting Armando")

You look up at the rooftop. It's a sniper. It's gotta be. You make like you're going to tie your bootlace and then start booking to the left. It's hard to run fast while halfway ducking too. Your back is stinging, but you keep running the best you can, always one step behind your shadow. The end of the block is in sight. There's a giant industrial looking mailbox there. If you could just hide behind it, no bullets could reach you. Damn, it's still about thirty feet away. Your soles slap against the sidewalk in staccato rhythms. Now it's twenty feet away. You can see the graffiti on it now, the code language of this foreign place. Your back is fucking burning. Your lungs ache. Your breath runs shallow. Goddamn! This shouldn't be that hard. It's like those nightmares where you're trying to run away and not getting anywhere. You're young. You should be able to commando-crawl faster than this! All you hear is your soles slapping against the cement, slowing down. Steel toes and Vibram soles are not what you need. That's for sure. At last, the mailbox. You slip behind it. You press your palm against it. The metal feels warm. The way you're breathing, you sound like a dog panting. You look intently at the lettering on the tag: the curves and twists of the letters, the sharp barbed wire like edges. It's angry, but it holds itself together like a family embracing. You get lost in the graffiti maze. At last your eyes dart away, only to see a wine colored trail from where you came. It must be your blood. Shit. You've been shot.

———————⟨⟩———————

This is a dead end.

Turn back to an earlier page and choose another path .

BACK UP

(continued from "Meeting Armando")

Y ou're thinking you're such an idiot. You're leading the snipers
to the van! You should just run and duck for cover. But instead,
you're practicing wilderness survival skills by slowly backing up
as if any sudden movement would trigger an attack. Or maybe you're
just a sitting duck for them. You just manage to stand next to the
van behind the extra large side-view mirror. Charlie's looking at you
funny. You have to warn him. You have to speak.

"Charlie, there's a sni..." At that moment, a bullet hits the concrete
near your feet. You open the door, but Charlie is already backing up
and turning so the next bullet could get him and not you. You're half
way in and trying to close the door, but it swings wide open.

"Hang on!" Tires screech like a million angry abuelas. Your leg is
hanging out and brushes against the pavement as the van continues its
turn. Your left hand is groping the air. You're gonna fall out! Just then
someone grabs your hand and you hold on goddamn fucking tight.
You hear bullets hit metal, then the roar of the engine as Charlie starts
hauling ass down the road. You tuck your leg in and close the door.

"Is anyone hit?" you ask.

"Not me."

"A-OK."

"That was crazy! We almost died! A bullet landed at my fucking
feet! I can't believe it!"

"Chela, put your seatbelt on." You look back, but Pato doesn't even have his on. He should take his own advice. The click of the belt is reassuring as buildings whiz by. No one should be following you.

"What do you think happened to little Armando?" you ask.

"Looks to me like there are only three options: he could be dead, kidnapped, or he was one of the motherfuckers shooting at us!" says Pato with authority.

"How do you know there was more than one shooter?" you wonder.

"Details, Chela, details." Fedi responds. "The bullets at your feet were from a rifle with a silencer, but the ones hitting the van were from a small gun that could have fit in a backpack."

"You really are from the hood, aren't you?"

"Damn straight!"

"Never straight, just sassy."

"Hey, will you guys shut up?" Charlie pipes in fiercely. "I need to pull over. We've been hit, you know!"

"If we're gonna blow up, I think we would have done it by now," sasses Fedi.

"I'm driving. I'm the only jerk here who knows where we are. So just shut up!" His face is all contorted, looking like a madman with that reddish stain on his collar. You feel a smile coming on in recalling your secret escapade.

The van screams around the next corner and then Charlie dramatically reduces the speed. You all creep along, going in slow-mo zigzag patterns. Finally, you arrive in some sleepy neighborhood, clearly working-class, but mellow. Charlie busts out the tool kit and systematically checks all the fluids in the vehicle. The bullets did go through the nose of the car, but seemed to miss the important parts of the engine. He tapes up a rubber hose with duct tape. You don't ask what it's for. Soon you're back on the road. "We have to go to a real mechanic. Just after our show tonight."

"How far is it to Green Sticks?" you ask.

"Palos Verdes? Like thirty, thirty-five miles. Why?"

"Remember I have a super important errand to run. I was supposed to be there yesterday."

"Oh, right. I think it's too late to go there today. It's 2:30 already."

"Too late?"

"Well, yeah. Traffic. This is L.A. County and we still need to get to La Colectiva, drop off some of our stuff, shower, check in at the club and drop off our instruments, eat, practice…"

"OK, OK. We'll go to Green Sticks tomorrow. I got his phone number. I'll call him on your *new* phone."

Turn to page 132.

THE HOUSE UPON THE HILL
(continued from "Crossing At Rush Hour")

You attempt to call Mr. Long from the bar. It's just past nine a.m. You get his message machine. "Hi, Mr. Long. I'm Chela, I mean Chavela from Mexico City. Well, I'm here in your town and ready to buy the bass from you. We can pick it up today if that's good. Please call me back." You hang up. Pato gestures to you from across the bar. You go to him. "What's up?"

"Who were you just talking to?"

"Mr. Long, the guy with the…"

"Yeah, I know who he is by now. What the *hell* are you doing?"

"What do you mean?"

"Don't you think he might notice the background bar noise? Don't you want him to respect you?"

"Doesn't *he* go to bars himself?"

"It's not the same!"

"Why not?"

"Because he's rich and you're like a foreign rag to him, ready to clean his toilet."

"No, I'm no rag to anyone here. I'm the *customer!*"

"That's what *you* think. You'll see. Just wait." You give him a bitter look.

"So what did he say?"

"He wasn't there, OK? He wasn't fucking there! I left a message,

129

a message with all kinds of background noise. Shit! What should we do now?"

"Whoa, slow down. You have his address, right?"

"Of course I have his address!"

"Let's get our asses over there before some other crazy shit happens! Know what I'm saying?"

"Damn, Pato, you're right! Our lives could spin in a million different directions in this place. I always thought I knew what to do or where to go next. I can't figure this place out. Feels like we could end up anywhere…"

"I'm not worrying about landing anywhere, Chela. I'm worried about ending up in the hands of the Migra or the po-po which are owned by the Migra these days!"

"I think I'd pick the Migra over some of these SoCal street gangs, but then again, I'd rather not hang with either!"

The ride along the coast is gorgeous. But instead of relaxing and taking in the air through the window, your stomach is all tore up. Must have been the greyhound you downed. The grapefruit juice had a metallic aftertaste. You rub your belly as you drift northward.

The road grows swervy and you start to gain elevation. You find yourself along a cliff with the ocean below. To the east is a rolling hodgepodge of hills with large estates on them. Charlie pulls over.

"Shit, I think I passed the turn-off," he says. You hear the chorus of moaning. "We'll have to double back."

At that, he pulls a U in the middle of the two-lane highway. You watch as the oncoming cars scramble not to hit you. Now the ocean is just over to your right. The three-hundred-foot drop seems to flatten and as you drape your hand outside the window, it seems you could reach down and cup the water.

"Hold on, guys!" Charlie warns and turns left, forcing you against oncoming traffic once more. Your stomach contents lurch upwards and pool in your mouth. The acrid concoction of booze mixed with sour juice and stomach acid burns as you swallow it back down. Great. All you need is to smell like a wino. Charlie starts climbing a hill and halts abruptly. There is a gate at a midpoint of the hill, forcing you all to stop and look up at the wonder that is his McMansion.

"There she is," Charlie announces and pushes the red button on the silver call box.

Turn to page 138.

THE PULSE

(continued from "Back Up")

The giant 3-D bleeding Aztec heart stands above the other buildings in the area. You see it from three blocks away.

"Hey, Chela, what did I tell ya? I wouldn't get us lost," Charlie boasts.

"This is so cool, yo, I can't believe we're here!" says Fedi. You sport a mild smile on your face. Pato says nothing. Charlie starts to park out front. A short, dark man emerges from the club in his pressed Dickies, chrome chain and punker-than-thou steel-toe boots.

"Hey, guys!" he says. "You're Los Húerfanos, right?"

"Yeah," Pato says almost protectively.

"I'm Jonny. I'm in charge of operations. Look, dudes, don't bother parking here, we have a loading zone over this way." He makes some gestures.

Charlie follows him to the side of the building where wide double-doors await. To a sheltered suburban housewife, the back of the club looks like a punk rock hellhole. The walls are layered with wheat-pasted posters and fresh graffiti and yet it's all hyper-real like an ad. Everything is perfectly highlighted and shaded. There's no broken glass, no garbage, no syringes. It's like a freaking hospital or something and that's just the *outside* of the building.

You all start lugging your equipment when Jonny and a team of short stocky guys intercept you. They insist on carrying everything. You wouldn't have needed Armando anyway. You follow them along an ample hallway lined with autographed posters of all the bands that have played there since its inception. At the end, there's an empty frame labeled by a little black and red plaque reading Los Huérfanos del D.F. He leads you to a green room, but it's more like a plush palace of green rooms compared to anything you all have ever seen, that is, except for Fedi, of course. There's a full spread of cheese, cold cuts, crackers, fruit, mini empanadas and taquitos dorados, beer and wine. You all pounce on it like feverish hyenas. Before long, Jonny is back and whisks Fedi and Pato away to talk business. When they return, you're all instructed to wash your hands and sign the Los Huérfanos del D.F. poster. Somebody must have photoshopped the photos from the press packet Pato sent. You wonder if they even attached your head to a different body or something. You don't remember wearing such tight clothes or looking so curvy in that Lowrider Magazine sort of way. Fedi, of course, is in front, way bigger than everyone else. The poster tells the story of how you're all rags-to-fame hooligans who had to make do by your wits in the crazy Mi Vida Loca slums of D.F. In the background, there's a wall with more hyper-real graffiti. Some of it is blurred for effect, making it even harder to decipher, but you swear it says Bang Data next to Fedi's face. Your stomach hurts again. You must have eaten too fast.

After the signing, you all go out to do an elaborate sound check. Fedi takes you aside and reminds you to keep your promise. You will *not* upstage him except for your prearranged solos.

"Hey, Chela, don't look so glum," Charlie starts. "We're *headlining!*" He puts his arm around your shoulder. You jerk in shock. This is the first time he's shown you any affection since the laundromat. Your eyes dart side to side to see if anybody's watching. You pull away.

"Aren't you gonna change out of that shirt?"

"Nah. I'm gonna cherish the memory a little longer if you don't mind."

"I guess." You halfway smile and then turn away. You gotta stay focused. You have an hour before the show. The boys go pig out some more while you find yourself pacing. There's nothing on your mind, absolutely nothing. You've drawn a blank, but the feelings are there brewing underneath, whatever they are.

You can't believe how many people show up. It's *packed!* Are they really coming to see Los Huérfanos or is it all about Fedi? Who knows, they could have hyped you all up all over town as some ghetto treasure not to be missed. You clamber up on stage. It feels strange, you can't see the audience, but you know there's a field of bobbing heads in front of you. Behind you are backdrops resembling urban streets. They even sketched out a fruit stand and a lady sitting on a box crocheting alongside two hoodlums playing cards. You want to ditch this fake-ass scenario and yet there's a part of you that loves it. You have urges to start miming begging for change just to see if the audience eats it up. But no, you go through your songs like a robot compared to your usual flare and stylings. Well, at least you're keeping your promise to Fedi and you're still probably more interesting than *most* bass players out there. Charlie and Fedi crack edgy jokes on stage in the usual swaggery punk rock fashion. "And on the bass we got Chela 'Don't mix the meat' Coatlicue!"

"Yeah, well at least I'm not a nun-lover like some barrio warrior I know!" you retort. He never explains what he originally meant by saying, "Don't mix the meat." It could have simply been about food or having more than one lover or going down on someone without first rinsing your mouth.

"Well at least I *know* who I love!" That was it. You uncoil your extra chord and shoot up in the front of the stage. You start rocking hard giving Les Claypool a run for his money. Your fingers are in a flurry like a guitarist. Your impromptu solo is fast and clear like metal, but twisty and tricky like jazz. There's a sassy tone to it. Fedi hates all that. The bass is for low and slow to drive the beat. But fuck it. You're not in some chain gang just trying to keep time. You gotta be free! You pluck out another driving flourish, an exclamation point to your sassy response then you set the bass down and dive into the audience. You don't give them much time to react and mobilize below. You almost hit the ground, but at the last minute they got you, a small bunch of fans, but they got you. Somehow in the commotion you notice one of the guys has only one arm, the other is a prosthetic with a hook. His one living arm is solid like a granite pillar. Fedi announces a small break. A bouncer comes out and shuffles you backstage to join your crew.

"You fucking bitch, Chela!" starts Fedi. "You promised..."

"Then don't start announcing my personal business all over town, you asshole."

"What's the big fucking deal? This is the twenty first century. Everybody's bisexual. It's cool *for women* especially!"

You put your hands on your cheeks and start screaming. Then you dive for Fedi's face. You start clawing at his neck. Pato and Charlie pry you off of him and start dragging you backward. You see Fedi's neck is bleeding. You might have ripped out an earring, scratched him too deep. Whatever.

"Yo, Chela, I know what he said was messed up, but try to calm down," says Charlie.

Pato starts rubbing your back. "It's OK, friend. It's OK. Hey, we can't have you disfiguring our best asset here. It's bad enough he's still healing from that tussle with Charlie."

You start to wriggle free of his embrace. You want to give it another go!

"Yeah, you want a piece of this? Alright then. Show me what you got!" Now Charlie leaves you to attend to Fedi.

"Try to think of something else," Pato says in a calm voice.

"That was quite some stage dive you managed. I thought you were going to bite it right there," says Charlie.

"We got good fans. They managed to catch me. Even the guy with the claw hand."

"What?" yelps Pato.

"Damn, really?" says Charlie. "Do you think it was the same dude we saw in Chicano Park?"

"The halfway invisible guy? Yeah, it was him. I'm sure of it."

"What the hell are you guys talking about? Tell me!" demands Pato.

Just then Jonny and his crew come in. "Hey, we need you back on stage. They're getting restless out here. They've been screaming for

135

more, but I'm afraid they're gonna get tired and either bail or tear up the place. Either way, I can't have it." He hustles you all back on stage.

During the second set you go back to being obedient. Fedi keeps turning his head back to check on you and when he does, you jerk like you're faking to take off up front again. Then he jerks and skips a note or two, but no one seems to notice. Oh well. You gaze over at Pato on the drums. You expect him to be giving you that stern father look, but instead, his eyes are wide. He looks sort of like the bull does when he knows his hours are numbered and he's begging for mercy. Pato wants something, bad. You keep playing. Fedi stops slamming you between songs and starts demonizing the one-percenters, literally. He says they're God's Devils in sheep's clothing or some shit while we're all the real lambs getting our bones sucked dry and not even realizing. Whether they understand him or not, the crowd bursts into hoots and cheers. Then Fedi busts out into some of the best solos yet. He really has become a master at guitar. Maybe finding God has helped him focus his gifts better…either that or he sold himself to the Devil in priest's clothing by accident.

The crowd is going ape-shit. You finish the set and are starting the first encore when you look back at Pato. His shoulders are covered in beads of sweat and his head and neck look downright soaked. His heart is not in it as he plays, but still the crowd hollers for more and you give it to them. After three encores, the emcee comes on stage and starts announcing upcoming events. You turn around to get off the stage and notice that Pato has already gone. You look for him backstage, in the green room and in the talent bathroom, but he's not anywhere. No one knows where he is. You try to run down the street, but there are so many fans milling about and they all want to talk to you and congratulate you. Finally, you break away. You start tearing down the streets of West Hollywood calling out his name. You don't know where you're going, you're just hoping to catch his scent. You swear you can smell him a couple of times. Somehow you're always one step behind, wherever you go. When the breeze picks up, confusing your nose, you just curl up behind an SUV and sob. The patterns of tread blur into a solid black, the most solid thing you got.

Turn to page 143.

BAIT AND SWITCH

(continued from "The House Upon The Hill")

A robotic sounding male voice emanates from the call box. You explain who you are and he buzzes you in. The driveway is steep and hedged by a monotonous sea of green lawn making the house seem even more impressive. At last you arrive at the large paved oval and park. The front door is built for Goliath. A handful of steps further distinguish the front door by having it stand even taller. A servant who opens the door is a middle-aged Latino man with perfect English. He wears a brown suit with a teal tie and cream-colored shirt. He looks like he could be a car parker at a fancy resort. His name is Gómez. You assume that's his last name if it is his name at all. As he speaks, you notice an echo. He leads you ruffians to a living room with a minimalist motif. You hear someone clear his throat. You whip around to see Mr. Long standing at the other side of the room. He's wearing gray tweed knickers and matching suit. A bass case lies before him.

"Hello, Chavela. Good to meet you at last."

"Great to meet you, too, Mr. Long."

"I'm impressed you came quite a distance…"

"We had a tour scheduled in the area."

"Yes, I recall. If you hadn't, I would have insisted on shipping it to you."

You swallow hard. Your throat is tightening up. "I thought on your ad it stated you would not ship internationally."

"Oh, did it? I guess it did. I could have been convinced, but since you had that gig lined up…how did it go anyhow?"

You're sure your tongue has doubled in size and is wedging itself within your throat. Pato talks for you.

"We actually decided to come here first. Our show is tonight. You're welcome to come…"

"That would be awesome. I'd love to get to know your guys better…but I have a plane to catch…"

"Oh," said Pato seeming interested. "Where will you be going?"

"Switzerland. I'm training for a triathlon. Instead of running, I'll be cross-country skiing."

"That's so amazing! I'm gonna do something like that one day!" You wondered how long Fedi was going to keep his mouth shut. "Doing extreme sports," he goes on "is one way to get closer to God." You notice Pato rolling his eyes. You have an urge to slap both of them.

"God? How is that?"

"Well, when doing extreme sports, you gotta push yourself right? I mean beyond anything normal. You gotta trespass the very limits of your body!"

"Ok, I'm following you…"

"So…who do you think helps you during those times of need? What keeps you going? If you think it's those power drinks or drugs or gooey food, you're wrong. It's God, of course, whether you know it or not! He's got you covered."

"Fascinating theory. So you do sports, do you?"

"Nah, but after this music business gets old, I'd like to swim up the coast of México. I have to call upon God for other things in my life; I mean just surviving the streets…you wouldn't believe what I been through and in the end, God got me floating on top." You can think of other things that end up floating on top…

"Oh, wait a minute. I know you. You're Federico, the one from Bang Data…"

"You got it. That's me…"

You can't believe it. He's upstaging you.

"I am familiar with your story. And you learned some English, too. Impressive."

"Hey, man, I'd love to talk about this more, but nature calls…"

"The restroom? Yes. Gómez will show you." The two of them walk off to the left and down a hallway.

"So, that leaves us to talk business. I'm assuming you have the cashier's check handy."

"Oh, yes, here it is." You had pulled it out during their philosophical conversation.

"I'm sorry, if you don't mind, I'd like to see your I.D. I guess a passport would be the thing."

You hand it over. He gives it a going-through-the-motions kind of look and leads you over to the bass. She is leaning against a wall. There is a light pointed right at her. It looks like she's a singer on stage or something. He opens the case and gestures for you to move in. Your heart's beating sounds like the snare drum roll. You peer into the case and gently remove her. The wood is nut brown just as you remembered. The texture, the shaping, the trimming all look so perfect. Too perfect. In the picture, The Lady had a rougher quality, something earthy, imperfect like Michelangelo's latter sculptures. You sniff around her neck, trying to look inconspicuous. It does smell like Opium perfume. The scent is harsh, but rounded, much like your grandmother's smell, but newer. In that intense lighting, she looks too perfect, too polished.

"Sir, do you mind if I take her into a different light?"

"Sure, she's yours now. Do as you will."

You let the remaining sunlight touch her. You find a chair and start playing. You bust out with the wild strumming intro to "Devil Blues." She sounds sweet. Crisp and deep with a nice balance of high tones. A fine instrument indeed.

"Wow, Chela," starts Charlie, "I didn't know you could play like that. Why aren't you off playing for something big-time?"

You look at him and shrug. "I like what we do. I…"

Out of nowhere, Fedi starts diving for The Lady. He snatches her out of your hands and smashes a hole in her body against a marble end table.

"What the hell are you doing?" you scream.

"Don't be fooled by this man!"

"Fedi, I'm going to fucking strangle you! You've lost it. You're batshit crazy!" He doesn't hear you. He's running back down the hallway toward the bathroom.

"I need you all to leave, *now*! Gómez, call the police!"

You put the broken Lady into her case. Your hands are shaking. Pato is standing between you and Mr. Long and Gómez. He won't let anyone touch you. Fedi reappears lugging another bass.

"This is the real thing you came for, Chela. Look at it. It's wild and raw like you…rough around the edges like you…but this, Chela, this bass knows God. I can feel it. This is the instrument you seek. Come on, let's get out of here away from these forked-tongued people."

You see Gómez whispering into Mr. Long's ear. Probably translating. At that, you all start to back up toward the door with Pato still flanking.

"You can't take that. That's *mine*!"

"Just stop, Mr. Long. She paid for it and you know it," says Pato.

You're halfway down the stairs when Pato walks out the front door. You all start running down the driveway. Charlie helps you lug the bass while Fedi struggles with his and Pato takes up the rear lookout. In the distance you hear sirens.

"Hurry!" calls out Charlie to the rest.

When you get to the gate, of course, it's locked.

"Don't worry, I got this." Fedi hands the bass to Pato, he takes a few steps back and dashes straight at the gate. At the last minute, he whips out his leg against the lock. You hear a loud pop and click and the gate opens. Fedi is a crumpled mess on the ground. Pato puts the bass in and carries Fedi. You're all in, but not seatbelted when Charlie pulls out, squealing down the road.

"Don't worry." Fedi says. "We'll get out of this."

"How do you know, man?" asks Pato.

"God told me. He told me other things, too, about this bass, Chela."

You can't speak. Your heart is beating out another drum roll. When the world was created, all that sounded was rhythm: rhythm for time unknown, until another sound trickled in. It was a cry, a cry of new life. A cry like a guitar, oozing in syrupy slow. Until the cry became clearer, with notes like glass. You hover there for a moment, until the euphoria dissipates and imperfections creep in. And the glass which once sounded so clear and God-like, cuts into your chest. Sirens! There are sirens surrounding you.

"Oh, shit!" belts out Charlie. "It's the po-po!"

Fedi slaps his forehead with his palm. "Slow down! We gotta pull over. We ain't outrunning nobody here!"

Charlie pulls over. His fingers look like bones clutching to the wheel. You look around at the white and black and red and blue pulsating collage that surrounds you. There must be over a dozen high-shouldered cops flanking every side of your car, even on the trail above the road.

"Fuck, man!" Fedi squeals. "We about to go down like some Brown Lives Don't Matter For Shit type 'a deal!"

"Where's your God, now?" you blurt out. "No fucking where."

"You don't know that, Chela! You don't fucking know shit!"

***

This is a dead end.

Turn back to an earlier page and choose another path

THE UNDERGROUND

(continued from "The Pulse")

"This is messed up!" Fedi hisses after hours of helping you look for Pato. "We're practically illegals here and bringing all this attention to ourselves is not cool…not at all. Fuck Pato, man…"

"Hey, don't you dis him!" you interject.

"Chela, you don't know because you split trying to find him, but we had a chance to get signed. There was an agent with Warner Brothers there, but it looked kinda bad that the two of you bounced and there was just me and Charlie standing there looking like two pendejos."

"Chill out, you two. You're bringing more attention to yourselves," Charlie says. "At least we got an awesome live recording. We can find someone else to produce it. There's still hope anyway. We got his card. He'll give us another chance…"

"Another chance? Barrio warriors like me don't get other chances. That's for rich kids like you. You get all the fucking chances in the world. What's that gringo expression…you get to eat oysters or some shit?"

"Hey, I've got an idea. There's an underground bar nearby. Let's check it out. If we don't find him there, we'll just go to La Colectiva and sleep there. Our rooms are ready."

"This is the last place I'm looking, Charlie, do you hear me? After this, I'm done."

You hope Pato is at this bar. You don't wanna end up hitting the streets by yourself again. It was making you feel kind of crazy, like you could feel him, but then he would drift away from you. Pato is not the type to heal his sorrows in bars and besides, if it's underground, how would he find it? Charlie leads you down a garbage-filled alley. You halfway expect a crew of zombie junkies to jump out at you. At the end of the alley behind an industrial dumpster are two big professional wrestler type guys in matching L.A. Angels hoodies.

Charlie waltzes up to them in his grubby ass T-shirt. "Hey, I'm looking for my patna' I suspect he's enjoying the facilities." The men are stone still. They don't even twitch a nostril.

Now Fedi toddles up. He speaks to them in Spanish. "Hey, yo, we're on tour and we lost our band member. He got spooked. We'd like to take a look around if we can. One of us can post it outside and wait."

"What band?" asks the thug on the right.

"Los Huérfanos del D.F. I'm Fedi. This is Chela and our gringo rhythm guitar player Charlie."

"Don't forget the clarinet!" Charlie pipes in.

"Los Huérfanos, eh?"

"Yeah, you've heard of us?"

"Maybe."

"Hey, TJ," says the one on the left. "This is the Fedi from Bang Data!"

"Oh, yeah, that's right, my cousin Turo went to that show. He said it was hella dope! Alright, we'll let you in, but *she* stays outside."

"Yeah," says the one on the left. Then he says with a smirk, "This is no place for a *lady*."

"Not this kind of lady, right ese?" At that they do some kind of wannabe Aztec arm shake. Great, now you're stuck outside with these door thugs. If Pato *is* in there, you're the one who would be able to get him out. *You* are his buddy. You start to drift over to the dumpster away from the guards.

"Hey, ruka, I wouldn't go back there."

"You're safer here with us."

"Don't worry, we're the good guys. The bad guys are out there." He points into the darkness. That's the guard on the right. You decide to call him Thug One.

You drag yourself back over toward the door. You try not to look at their faces. You just don't want to engage. You notice their shoes, glowing white under the black light. You figure they probably glow plenty in the daylight. Spotless white puffy sports shoes are a trend you never understood. You see movement over to your left. A cockroach scurries behind a cigar butt. There's no other garbage in the near vicinity of the door. It looks like somebody scrubbed the asphalt clean.

"So, what's it like to go on tour with all dudes?" asks Thug One.

"It's OK."

"Really? You fit in?"

"I fit in Enough."

"Come on, you can tell us the truth. They stink and they cuss and they say things about bitches you never wanted to hear!" says Thug One.

You shrug. "It's not that bad."

"Ever thought of being in a girl band?"

You look at them blankly.

"Cuz we could hook you up over here in L.A." Thug One offers.

"Yeah, we got mad connections," chimes in Thug Two.

"Girl bands are in," Thug One says.

"Girl bands are hot," adds Thug Two.

"I stay over in Mexico City…" You start to tell them.

"You *did* stay in Mexico City, but you aren't there now, ruka."

"But that's where I'm from. My family's there."

"Sure, that's where your *blood* family is, but you could *choose* a new family anywhere you go, esa." Thug One tells you.

"A family is what you make it," Thug Two adds.

"You could make something of yourself out here, Chela." Thug One says.

"Yeah, just lose a little weight and do something with that hair…", Thug Two adds.

"What the fuck? I don't need to lose weight!"

"Hey, girl, this is L.A. You're female and even if you're punk as fuck you gotta compete with all those 90210 types to get a hold of some producer's cojones," explains Thug Two.

"We could hook you up!"

"Just leave me the fuck alone. Don't talk to me."

"Oh, look who's getting all ghetto on us!" says Thug Two.

You feel the anger molting up inside you. You wanna kick something. You start stomping on a cockroach, but the mother-fucker won't die. The thugs are laughing at you. Just then, there's a knock from the inside of the door; Charlie and Fedi come out of the building.

"What the hell are you doing?" asks Fedi.

"Don't any of you fucking talk to me." You start to walk away toward the dumpster.

"Not even me?" It's Pato. You turn around and hug the shit out of him. He fucking reeks of sugar-sweet liquor, barf and cigar smoke. Great, this was the last clean shirt you had. The pants you've been recycling for some time. You figure his blood sugar must be off the charts.

"Hey, Pato, dude you need to drink some water. And we gotta check your sugars."

He doesn't say anything and now you wanna kick him, too. You look back and the cockroach is long gone. Fucking indestructible bastard.

Turn to page 147.

GREEN STICKS

(continued from "The Underground")

It's one o'clock in the afternoon by the time you wake up. The guys are all asleep. Fuck, you're two days late to pick up the Perfumed Lady. The air smells like nectar. You turn to Pato to make sure he's still breathing. He is. Who knows how high his blood sugar hit? You have a fear of witnessing people dead in their sleep. All your life you had a repeating dream of your grandmother Sálome near dead in her bed.

The covers are drawn up to her chin. You sit at her side, her bust out like naked bones, with the sides of her face clinging inward. There had been a candle lit on her dresser that dripped down into a warm puddle of white wax. You hear a persistent tapping. There is a hummingbird rapping on the window across from her bed. You watch this tiny flash of green and red hit the four corners of the window and then disappear. Your focus shifts back to abuela Sálome when you hear a piercing thud against the window. You open it and look around. Nothing. Then you gaze downward to see the hummingbird on the ground. It looks brown and plain and broken.

The last time you saw her living, was in this dream and it has clung to you since. You can never wipe it from your mind. If only Pato controlled his sugar better, then maybe you could let it slide like hot butter out of your brain. Instead, her face lingers...the bones...the tapping...the tapping.

You start packing your things frantically, making noise. You are feeling nervous about The Lady. It could already be too late. Despite your clamoring, the guys continue to snore. You leave the sleeping logs and wander into the kitchen of this punk rock arts collective. There you meet Matilda or Matti. She makes you some coffee with honey. You prefer sugar, but the honey works. She starts to give you a tour of the place. There are two different rooms dedicated to art, one focusing on crafts and the other, photography and movie making. She smiles and speaks to you in perfect Spanish, "You've got a lot on your mind, don't you?"

"How did you know?"

"Well, I figured the clenched fists were a good indicator. What's up? You wanna talk about it?"

"There's somewhere I need to go. But the guys are gonna sleep for another day and a half! Lazy bums!"

"Where? Is it far?"

"I think so." You swallow and then tell her your story. "There's a man in Palos Verdes who has a very special instrument that I think belonged to my grandmother. I want it back. He's agreed to sell it to me by the day before yesterday."

"I'll take you. I'm unemployed right now. Better this than waste my afternoon online."

You thank her numbly and rush back into the dormitory. You start rifling through your big bag to get your small bag, the one with your big money to pay for The Lady. You're just about to leave, when you hear Pato grumble. "Chela, wait. I'm coming." Slowly he forms his body into a crawling pose then pushes his chest and head up and at last, straightens the rest of his legs. "You need back-up. You don't know what this Mr. Long is about."

The three of you pile into Matti's 1980s biodiesel Mercedes and take off. The traffic is maddening. "God damn, why don't you all do what we do in Mexico City and ration which days you can drive. This is nuts! Why do you people need to be out on the road now…when we do!" you scream out.

"That's not going to help, Chela," Pato interjects.

"What, rationing?"

"No, you screaming! Screaming's not gonna get us there any faster!"

"Shut up!"

Matti ignores your bantering and plays the role of helpful tour guide. Her comments about the neighborhoods and historical tidbits help pass the time. At last you arrive in front of the Long McMansion up on a hill overlooking the cliffs and the ocean. There's a long driveway followed by a gate with a callbox followed by another long driveway surrounded by what seems like acres of plush green lawn. To the left of the callbox is a large white sign with lustrous red letters that reads: "For Sale."

"Shit! We're too fucking late! He better be home." You push the call button. No answer. Your throat is caving in.

"Chela, do you have the phone Charlie brought? Let's call the guy."

"Uh no, I left it at the collective. I can't believe I fucked this up!"

"Stop. Chela, we don't know that."

"You can use my phone. Here. I have the unlimited calling, *nationally*."

"Thanks, Matti, you rock!" You dig out the scrap of paper with Mr. Long's number. "OK, here we go." You press "Send." His voicemail pops up right away. You leave a message.

"Let's wait here," Matti suggests. "Besides, the traffic is going to be just as bad going back. Let's hang here, call him back and if he doesn't show up, then I know of a beach not too far away. We can go there and have ritual catharsis or something."

"Huh?"

"I mean, go to the beach and scream our heads off or throw rocks into the ocean or whatever."

You slump down beneath the callbox as if your presence would make it speak to you. No such luck. Pato and Matti start chatting and getting acquainted. You have your head between your knees. After a while you call back. Still no answer. You press the callbox a few times. Nothing.

"You know, I just wanna go up there and knock on that door. Maybe he's in there."

"I doubt it, Chela. We've been camped out here for over an hour," says Pato.

"Or I could go up and look through the windows to see if the Perfumed Lady is in there…"

Matti looks at you with her large green eyes. Her face holds an expression of saint-like compassion. You try to hold back your repulsion.

"I don't think that's such a good idea," she says at last. "People might think you're a robber."

"What? I'm not a robber. He stole this from me!"

"Well, he didn't actually steal it from you directly, Chela. You never had this instrument in your hands. Who knows the story of how it got onto the market? Maybe your grandmother needed some fast money. It might not be so messed up as you think.

You're shocked. What a traitor! "I wanna go up there, Pato."

"Chela, I'm telling you. It's a bad idea."

"But we came all this way and now I'm so close. How can I just sit here! How?"

"How about this, let's stay a few days and see if we can get a hold of him. Maybe we can sic Fedi on the internet trail and find out a different number for him…."

"We can't stay here. Don't we have other gigs? I just want to see if the house is empty. Don't worry. It's not like I'm going to break in if I see her."

"Really, Chela? If you saw the Perfumed Lady right there calling to you and hissing, 'Play me, child of my inheritance. Play me and set me free' you wouldn't go smash 'n grab?"

"That's not my style Pato."

"One thing that's really not your style would be: vicious guard dogs trying to get a bit of your juicy nalgas. I'm just saying…"

"If there were dogs, they'd have been barking at us by now, right?"

"There's no guarantee. They could be out back chillin' till they hear you steppin' up the driveway. They're saving all their energy to chomp on some burglar butt. Come on, let's go to the beach. It's nearby right?'

"Yeah, public access is three miles from here. That's close for L.A." Matti shares.

"OK, Chela, so there's a plan: we go to the beach and chill out and then come back. Maybe he'll have come back by then to take care of things. Maybe he's still at work now."

"We don't even know that he has a job. He's planning on retiring in his thirties in some other country."

"Well maybe he's shopping, Chela. Shopping for his trip."

Matti starts whistling.

"What are you doing *that* for?" asks Pato.

"I'm trying to call out the dogs."

"Don't humor her. She's super impulsive!"

If you decide to jump the fence to peer into the long mission,
turn to page 152

If you choose to go to the beach with Pato,
turn to page 154.

JUMP THE FENCE

(continued from "Green Sticks")

"**S**ee, there's no dogs. I'm doing this!" At that, you start scaling the fence. You manage fifteen inches of upward movement before you start slipping down.

"Ay, Chavela. Here, I'll give you a boost." Pato looks around before offering up his clasped hands. You hop on over to the other side. The fence looks so tall, so final. You're in Long's land now. You have no one to give you a boost back out. If there are dogs, you're screwed. You're not sure how to walk up the driveway, quietly or casually. People can see you from miles around. The house is a lookout post on a hill. You're shoulder-deep in gringo territory. Though you're itching to run, you go for a casual non-stomping stride. At least Pato and Matti have your back, in a way…the driveway is so long that soon there would be little they could do but scream out a warning.

You listen for sounds of panting or gnawing or grunting or buttons being pushed, but all you hear are the sounds of cars driving and the breeze. You wonder if these are the famed "Santa Ana" winds, the ones that turn sparks into wildfires. General Santa Ana, before losing The Alamo, kicked some major gringo ass. He could never have jumped sides like the American-made movies make it out. He would never sign the treaty willingly to give up almost half of México, if he signed at all…but then again, that's what winds do: they jump, they swirl in one direction then another…their loyalties waver. Does his windy spirit help you or hurt you now? It could be tricking your ears. You hear no dogs. You hear only the wind. As you draw near, you feel like a wildfire jumping boundaries, getting ahead of yourself, doing things just beyond your character profile.

You hear a high-pitched intermittent sound like a piccolo twisted by the wind. You look around, but you can't figure it out. You continue walking forward then up the front stairs. Next comes a giant circular landing and finally the house. You look *up* at the front windows. They are so far off the ground. Fuck! You make it to the front door. It's made of some kind of fancy wood with leaded glass slats. You press your face against one of them. It's hard to see anything but the empty entryway. If you climb onto the railing and stretch out, you could probably manage to shove your face into one of the front windows. Otherwise, you'll have to go to the back of the place, which really would feel more like you're an invader. Plus, what if there are dogs back there? The whistling continues faintly. You pull yourself up on top of the railing and shuffle your feet sideways. Almost to the window. You swing your left hand out and grip the window ledge. You're craning your neck to reach, but you can't quite make it. You're afraid you're going to lose your balance if you take another step. You've got to. You shift your weight to your right foot then lift your left...

"Don't move," says a man's voice. "Drop to the ground." You hesitate. "Do it!" You do. You turn your head to see a police officer. "This is private property, young lady, and you're breaking and entering."

"It's just that..."

"Put your hands in front of you."

He cuffs you. "You have the right to remain silent..."

Silent you will never be. Your flames will hiss. Your course is wild. You'll burn through restraints and anything trying to contain you.

This is a dead end.

Turn back to an earlier page and choose another path.

PATO AND THE BEACH
(continued from "Green Sticks")

"**O**K, fine, let's just get out of here."

You enter the car like a robot. You can't believe you're leaving. As you edge atop the coastline cliffs, the house on the hill shrinks down. Matti knows the way to some awesome beaches. She pulls up to a cliff's edge. The Pacific is raging in front of you, white and foamy. She leads you to a wooden stairway down the cliff. The three of you descend. Matti rattles on about the local history of the area. You barely hear her this time. It is cool, though, that she knows so much. She's good people. Better reason not to throw a tantrum, though you sure want to about now.

When you get to the bottom, you follow Matti's lead in taking off your boots. Pato doesn't. His feet are often sensitive…something to do with his diabetes. The sand is cool and firm. Matti stops playing tour guide and you all look out at the ocean. To you it's a raging titan ready to swallow up any passersby. You look over at Pato; his eyes are all dreamy-like, big and wet. Then you notice the beginnings of a tear welling up. "Pato, what's up?"

"I saw him Chela, OK?"

"Who? What are you talking about?"

"Mi Papá. I saw him at the show! He was there. He *knew* we were coming!" Matti starts to wander down the beach. "I went after him, Chela. That's why I disappeared."

"I thought you said he was dead."

"Dead to me, yeah. Dead after what he did."

You break the silence. "Well, did you talk to him?"

"Yeah, I did. I didn't have much to say. I mostly listened to his crap."

"What did he say?"

"He said he loved me and how he never wanted to leave and all that. He says he didn't call or send us word because he is in trouble with the law…big-time. He's got the fat cats after him, FBI, CIA and shit. He's in it real deep. It's gnarly, but he even had to cut off…"

"Hey, guys, I just got a text. It must be from Mr. Long. Sorry, Chela, it looks like he already sold it."

"What? What does it say?"

Matti sighs. "It says, 'You came too late. I was moving out of the country, had to sell fast. Sorry. Mr. L.'"

You find yourself screaming and running down the beach. Running, running right on the edge of the water, a splashy white trail behind you. You look at the gargantuan waves, wishing they'd gather a shitload of power to leap up the mountainside all the way into *his* house, just to swallow him whole. What a fucker! Who had The Lady now?

This is a dead end.

Turn back to an earlier page and choose another path

EPILOGUE

In the end, you always found yourself judging those old timers. You know, the ones that hang out out behind the plaza at night with the shiny cheeks and the swollen noses, talking about the same things... talking about the past like a swirl of ribbons in the wind entangled, swaying together, sometimes struggling to get free. "If only things were different..." "If I hadn't lost that money..." "If only...If only..." Always down for a good story, you listen for awhile until the repetition makes your skin itch. *Just move on!* you want to blurt out. Siempre pa'lante nunca pa'tras; always forward and never back! To you, life is made up of a series of choices. You don't believe in all that fate and destiny shit. Not anymore. Seems like people get the fever to make the same bad choice over and over like your cousin Silvia, who kept having babies with that broke-ass, abusive loser. Others get trapped by fear, even when they know what they're supposed to do. They just stand there and watch, as their opportunities wither away like cut flowers in a dry vase. That's you. Fedi was right. You are a chicken shit. You can't manage to stand up for your loved ones, let alone for yourself. If you had, maybe your grandmother would still be alive. If you had, you'd be a famous classical musician by now. Your mother's eyes would sparkle again. You never would have needed to chase after The Lady and lose yourself in northern lands.

If only you could start over and choose to be the personal assistant to that rich banker friend of your uncle. If only...if only.... You're adrift in a haze of time and space, maybe like those old timers. Yes, maybe like them.

GUIDE TO CHOICES

They say, "There's no turning back in life..." but not with this book. This book is about getting the opportunity for a redo. This guide is meant to help you turn back to the chapters that contain choices so you can make different ones.

WORK SHEET

Below you will find a list of the chapters with their corresponding page numbers in alphabetical order. The list is in alphabetical order so as not to spoil the plot. The author offers her help in keeping track of the chapters you've read. Feel free to cross off the chapters here as you read them. In doing so, you will have an idea of which chapters have not yet been read. If you read the majority of the book, you will find clues to answer many of your lingering questions.

GRATITUDES

B iggest thanks to my daughter, Estela! Giant hugs to all those who helped me take care of her while I was writing the first draft, Rachel, Julie, Dani, Mom, Becky, Andrea, Toby and Silvia. Thanks for your kind words and encouragement, Papi Waldo, Burrell Spites, Maya, Lauren, Kotechis family and James. And thanks to Pablo, James and Stewart for being plot collaborators. Thank you John Selawsky and Melanie Neale for editing support and conceptual advice.

Swimming Upstream: A Novel
Jacob Anderson-Minshall

Trans Homo…Gasp!
Gay FTM and Cisgender Men on Sex and Love
Avi Ben -Zeev and Pete Bailey

Lou Sullivan
Daring To Be A Man Among Men
Brice D. Smith

Trunky (Transgender Junky)
A Memoir of Institutionalization and Southern Hospitality
(Lambda Literary Finalist)
Sam Petersoon

Life Beyond My Body
Transgender Journey to Manhood in China
(Lambda Literary Award)
Lei Ming

Words of Fire!
Women Loving Women in Latin America
Antonia Amprino

Trunky (Transgender Junky)
A Memoir of Institutionalization and Southern Hospitality
Sam Peterson

Queer Rock Love: A Family Memoir
Paige Schilt

I Know Who You Are, But What Am I?
A Partner's Memoir of Transgender Love
Ali Sands

Love Always
Partners of Trans People on Intimacy, Challenge, and Resilience
Edited by Jordon Johnson and Becky Garrison

Real Talk for Teens:
Jump-Start Guide to Gender Transitioning and Beyond
Seth Jamison Rainess

Now What?
A Handbook for Families with Transgender Children
Rex Butt

New Girl Blues...or Pinks
Mary Degroat Ross

Letters for My Sisters: Transitional Wisdom in Retrospect
Edited by Andrea James and Deanne Thornton

Manning Up: Transsexual Men on
Finding Brotherhood, Family and Themselves
Edited by Zander Keig and Mitch Kellaway

Hung Jury: Testimonies of Genital Surgery by Transsexual Men
Edited by Trystan Theosophus Cotten

Below the Belt: Genital Talk by Men of Trans Experience
Edited by Trystan Theosophus Cotten

Giving It Raw: Nearly 30 Years with AIDS
Francisco Ibañez-Carrasco

166

Made in the USA
Columbia, SC
17 December 2018